HILLSIDE ENCOUNTER

Other books by Shelagh McEachern:

Mr. Perfect

HILLSIDE ENCOUNTER

•

Shelagh McEachern

AVALON BOOKS
NEW YORK

PRINTED IN THE UNITED STATES OF AMERICA
ON ACID-FREE PAPER
BY HADDON CRAFTSMEN, BLOOMSBURG, PENNSYLVANIA

Chapter One

The helicopter didn't disappear.

It circled and landed.

Julie recognized the green logo as property of Tracklin's, the powerful logging company, the major employer in this wilderness area. She didn't trust that name; Daniel had warned her they put profits before people. She couldn't imagine why it was landing here so far from anywhere.

The tall pilot stepped out of the helicopter, dark glasses covered his eyes, but nothing could hide his confident stance and the arrogant lift of his chin. He surveyed the hillside with an air of ownership.

Julie bristled and rose to her feet, brushing the dried grass and dirt from her knees. Her eyes narrowed as she glared at the long dark shadow outlined on the grassy hillside. Visitors were rare in these parts, and judging from the length of his shadow, this one was huge. She squinted into the bright sunshine to get a closer look at his features but all she could clearly see were golden glints of sun-streaked blond hair. She had definitely never met this man before.

The curious children gathered around her, their berry buckets clanking together as they also stared into the sun at the stranger striding toward them, smiling in greeting.

The pilot had the advantage of the sun behind him, so was able to take in the woman's soft brown eyes under long dark lashes following his movements suspiciously. She was a beauty, standing in a tangled field with leafy bits and a single white daisy sticking out of her mass of curly dark hair; but she didn't return his smile.

Undeterred, he removed his sunglasses and stared directly into her lovely face. She seemed reluctant to accept his presence here, perhaps even angry at his intrusion, but he couldn't imagine why. Tracklin's owned timber rights on this land; he wasn't trespassing, he was entitled to be surveying it, but judging from the way she was glaring at him, he was not welcome.

His smile widened and took in the three children. "Hello. From the air, it looked like you were having fun. What are you picking?"

The voice was deep and seductive but Julie was having none of it. He may have dazzling blue eyes and a megawatt smile but he was part of the logging company that did so much damage in these woods. His charming smile couldn't undo that. She pursed her lips, holding back all those scathing remarks about lumber barons destroying the environment. She must remember that she was only a guest here, and mustn't make life difficult for her sister's family by enraging the neighbors. Sweet Moira, in her seven-year-old innocence, beamed at the man, making up for Julie's lack of manners, and answered, "We're picking bramble berries. Look," she gestured as she stepped closer, "we've picked lots."

His smile welcomed the little girl, angelic as she stood in the tall grass, haloed by the sunshine. She had his undivided attention. "I'm not familiar with brambles, they look a bit like blackberries. May I taste one?"

The guy was a charmer, all right. Before Moira could open her mouth, Simon had rushed up to the stranger's side holding out his berry bucket. "Here, take one of mine. I picked them myself." He beamed as the tall man bent down and sampled one of the offered berries.

"Mmm. Very good. What will you do with them all?"

"Mommy makes jam," said Simon.

"And bakes pies," Moira added.

The intruder was working his magic on the children but Julie was not as trusting. Although she loved every curl on Simon's three-year-old head, now was not the time to be so endearing. This man had the wealth and power to clear-cut this entire hillside and never think of the family living here. With frosty gaze, she watched him chatting with her niece and nephews. *He probably ate little children for breakfast.*

Shyness gone, the children talked nonstop, warmly welcoming the stranger in their midst. They were too young to be suspicious, even nine-year-old Jake, usually cautious about newcomers, joined in, overwhelming the man with questions about the helicopter.

"Could we go up close . . . look at the controls?"

Julie still stood apart in the patch of brambles. It could be a Greek god dropped from the sky, the way the children were carrying on. She was not so innocent or so trusting. That Tracklin logo meant power . . . and trouble. "A ruthless machine," Daniel had said. "Profits before people." She didn't want to encourage the likes of him, but he included her in his generous smile and stepped closer.

Unused to women reacting with such cool distrust, the pilot was curious. This woman wasn't shy, as he'd first thought. She was hostile. What had he done to offend her? Her children were friendly, why was she frowning at him?

He rose to his full height, towering over her, blocking the sun, casting a shadow over her sun-bronzed face. He smiled then, especially for her. It was a beautiful smile that did strange things to Julie's insides. He could probably charm mermaids out of the sea, but she wasn't falling for it. With much effort, she maintained her composure.

His voice was as beguiling as one would expect from a charmer. He extended his hand. "I'm Andrew Tracklin; I was inspecting the standing timber." Julie shook his hand politely and nodded.

"Surely, you're not thinking of logging this beautiful hillside, Mr. Tracklin?"

So, she had a voice . . . husky and melodic . . . and filled with protest. "A little selective logging may increase its beauty."

He must have said that to get a reaction . . . and he wasn't disappointed. Julie scowled, thinking of all the bald mountainsides she'd seen after ruthless logging. Her voice was strangled somewhere in her throat.

He didn't give her time to lecture him on ecological logging practices . . . he smiled that megawatt smile and asked, "Would you mind if I showed the children the helicopter?"

Julie swallowed. The children looked up at her with such hopeful anticipation, she couldn't disappoint them. She struggled to keep her voice civil, she even managed a slight smile. "They'd like that."

It was only three words, but with a quiet gentleness he would remember.

He nodded, acknowledging her permission. She didn't seem anxious to engage in any lengthy conversation and the three excited children had set off skipping across the clearing. He hastened to catch up with them.

As Julie watched the children, bubbling with questions, an indulgent smile turned up the corners of her mouth. Her wary eyes followed their movements.

Turning to follow the children, the pilot caught that smile on Julie's face from the corner of his eye. She was a delight—as natural and dazzling as the sun in the clear blue sky, wholesome and fresh, nothing artificial. He was startled by his reaction, turned quickly, and sauntered off to catch up with the children.

After they inspected the helicopter and each sat in the

pilot's seat, the three were sent scampering back across the field to Julie. The handsome pilot watched until they were beside her, waved, then stepped inside the cockpit. The children waved vigorously, happy faces turned to the sky as the helicopter roared to life, lifted, dipped to the east, then disappeared over the hilltop.

"Julie, you should've seen inside. It was neat!"

"Yeah. He let us wear his helmet." Moira's soft eyes studied her aunt. "You thought he was nice, too, didn't you Julie?"

If you went for tall, athletic men with golden tans and dazzling blue eyes, you could say he was nice. Moira's trusting face still watched her aunt, so Julie lied. "Of course I thought he was nice. Not every man would show three nosy children his helicopter." The little girl grinned.

"I was scared," Simon whispered. "Moira held my hand, and the man promised not to start the motor until I was back with you. It's good to keep promises, isn't it?"

Julie bent down to hug her nephew and tousle his unruly hair, as tightly curled as her own. "Yes, Simon, it is." She wanted to say something to caution them against trusting a Tracklin but she could see she was outnumbered by these three new members of the Tracklin Fan Club.

Thankfully, Jake changed the subject. "I'm starving. Can we eat now?"

They lay back in the tall grass, sun warming their faces as they devoured the picnic lunch. The blue sky was cloudless, the berry buckets were filled, her sister, Anna, was recovering nicely and Daniel's fishing was successful. It was summer, filled with lush growth and the promise of a bountiful harvest.

Julie stared into the sky remembering the phone call from her brother-in-law only a few weeks ago. She was sitting in her west end condo studying the glossy travel brochures, anticipating her vacation in Hawaii.

Daniel's voice was stricken; he had trouble forming the words, "Anna has fallen."

"How serious is it?"

"Pretty bad, Julie . . . she's broken her arm and leg." Julie gasped as Daniel continued, "She slipped on wet seaweed and went over the bank onto jagged rocks." She could hear him inhaling, trying to pull himself together.

"Have you managed to get her to a doctor?"

"We brought the boat to Powell River . . . she's in the hospital. Julie, she was in terrible pain . . . she didn't complain . . . the children are in shock . . ."

Julie could hear the unanswered questions: *What will we do now? Who will look after Anna, care for the children, tend the gardens and the animals? A man as fiercely independent and self-sufficient as Daniel must be having a difficult time making this phone call.* Julie didn't hesitate. "I have a three-month leave of absence, Daniel, I'll be there in four days."

A sigh of relief traveled down the phone lines. "The children and I have to get back to Desolation Sound before nightfall—the animals need to be fed."

"I'm coming, Daniel. Meet me at the ferry in Powell River on Tuesday. Do you suppose Anna can be released from the hospital by then?"

"I think so, Julie. She wanted to come home with us today . . . she's had her arm and leg set . . . they're in casts . . . the doctor wouldn't hear of it."

"Take care of yourself and the children; I'll be there as fast as I can."

"Julie . . ." She thought the line was dead, but he added on a whisper, "Thanks."

"Don't thank me yet, Daniel. This city girl doesn't have any of Anna's homesteading skills . . . but I'll give it my best shot."

So here she was.

Although she should be carefree, not a worry to mar the

sunny day, Julie shivered. Something about her encounter with that Tracklin man left her feeling on edge. She couldn't quite identify it, but a strange uneasiness haunted her as the happy troupe trudged down the hillside heading home to prepare dinner.

The pilot ate his solitary dinner at the lumber camp, still troubled over the scene on the hillside where he was so obviously not welcome.

What was bothering that woman? He couldn't get her out of his mind . . . mysterious, wild, and distant . . . who was she?

Noticing him lost in thought, the camp manager approached his table. "Being boss too much for you?"

The young man grinned at the gruff question. "Not yet," he replied, glad to see Bruce Sorkin. He offered him a seat at his table; Bruce had been here a long while and knew all the goings on in the area, he'd know who that woman was.

"I flew over the area David marked for spraying this afternoon, checking for signs of moth, caterpillar or insect damage. I couldn't see anything." The older man's friendly face encouraged him.

"I did see a woman and three children picking berries, so I landed to be neighborly." He paused, shrugging his broad shoulders, carefully choosing his words. "I didn't get a warm welcome."

As Bruce raised his eyebrows, he explained further. "Oh, the children were friendly . . . but the woman was not pleased to see me . . . hostile, even."

"Scared them, did you?"

"More than that. She glared as if I were the devil in person. Since when is a neighborly visit around here greeted with coldness? What's going on, Bruce?"

The camp manager hesitated, staring intently at his hands.

The pilot noticed. He exhaled and leaned back in his chair, the remains of his dinner pushed aside. His voice was whisper soft. "Has my big brother, David, been throwing his weight around?"

Bruce Sorkin dodged the question. "It had to be Anna Corwin. Three children with her . . . two boys and a girl?"

"That's right."

"The Corwins have fifteen acres on Desolation Sound, been there ten years . . . cozy subsistence farm. Daniel fishes and plants trees for the cash they need. Mostly they provide for themselves. Both Daniel and Anna are painters. They wanted to raise a family away from the violence and pollution of the city, give them an appreciation of nature and live in harmony with the land.

"I was skeptical at first, idealistic and dreamy, I thought. They'll never last. But they work hard; they made a go of it. You have to respect people who practice what they believe. It can't be easy living so cut off from people and without modern conveniences." Bruce stroked his chin with his thumb. "A nice family—the Corwins."

He couldn't see any hardships daunting that woman on the hillside. He guessed she would take on anything. He wondered about her husband, dealing with a wife like that every second of the day, no escaping to the office.

Bruce Sorkin's gruff voice cut off his wandering thoughts. "Daniel's the best tree planter in the lot. Many quit, can't take the isolation, but Daniel's dependable." Bruce stroked his whiskered chin, pondering Tracklin's meeting with Daniel's family.

"Anna Corwin wouldn't be unsociable—gentle girl, devoted mother, concerned about the environment." He shook his head. "I couldn't imagine her being hostile."

The concern on his employer's face didn't ease. "Sure you weren't reading more into it than was there?"

"No, Bruce. I saw what I saw. That was no gentle loving creature on the hillside—the woman bristled at the sight of me."

The last was said so forcefully, Bruce didn't dare to argue. "Strange," he muttered. "I haven't seen the Corwins for months. They keep pretty much to themselves. But that doesn't sound like Anna."

He thumped the younger man on his shoulder. "Tell you what, Daniel will be in tree planting next week, I'll see what I can find out."

Not wishing to stir up trouble for a homesteading family who probably needed all the support they could get, Andrew Tracklin sighed dramatically, drawing attention away from the Corwins. "Rejection always hurts."

Bruce guffawed, a wide grin creasing his weathered face. "I'll wager women don't often give you the cold shoulder."

Although he was trying to appear devastated, the laugh lines deepening around Andrew's eyes gave him away. Both men laughed. Then Bruce let slip a little more than he intended. "You're human, a good boss needs a heart. Men don't respect a machine."

Mr. Tracklin's eyebrows rose, he was quick to pick up the implication. "Has David alienated the men?"

Those intense blue eyes urged him on. "David wants to modernize, make changes, replace men with machines. Men aren't enthusiastic about losing their jobs. But David wants efficiency, production . . . can't blame him for that. Your father drilled it into him." Bruce pressed his lips shut, reluctant to say more. After all, Tracklin's was his employer, paid his wages, he couldn't risk losing his job.

Andrew Tracklin furrowed his brow. "I want to hear the whole story. I can't run a company, even briefly, if I'm kept in the dark."

Bruce trusted the younger Tracklin son and felt safe revealing the list of complaints. "The men think David's too ambitious, puts profits before safety. There's grumbling in the camp." Bruce looked Andrew squarely in the face. "I'm

glad you stepped in. A strike would close down the woods,
put a lot of men out of work."

"How do the men feel now?"

"Things are quiet. Everyone is giving you a chance to
prove yourself." He shifted his weight on his chair. "If David stepped back into the office tomorrow, mark my words,
strike talk would be back in the air."

The situation was volatile. The somber expression on
Andrew Tracklin's face revealed its seriousness.

Both men stood. Andrew shook the camp manager's
hand. "Thanks for leveling with me. That encounter on the
hillside had a positive outcome after all. Mrs. Corwin did
me a favor . . . let me know Tracklin's is making enemies."
He wasn't taking the problem lightly, there was determination in his voice. "I'll have to work at changing that."

Bruce Sorkin watched his boss walk away. He had a big
job ahead of him, but if Andrew Tracklin stayed around a
bit longer, he was just the man to do it.

He looked neither left nor right. Miraculously, a path
cleared to the exit.

Perhaps because he was taller than the average traveler
in Vancouver Airport, or because he had an air of authority,
the crowds parted, and he continued across the airport
lounge in long, casual strides. Heads turned and admiring
eyes followed him.

The airport hummed with noise and frenzied activity, but
his pace was unhurried.

He stood out in the crowd—a handsome man with riv-
eting blue eyes, firm jaw and sun-streaked hair. Mere mor-
tals couldn't look that stunning.

With flight bag in hand, he calmly proceeded through
the crush of people pushing luggage carts or staring at mon-
itors. Andrew Tracklin continued through the exit doors,
past waiting taxis, into a shuttle that took him to the crew

parking lot. The cool blue eyes, nerveless and confident in the cockpit, now sparkled with anticipation and curiosity.

Why the urgent summons? What required his presence? The message from his mother was a mystery. It was unlikely to be business; his father and brother took care of the Tracklin Empire. He'd been filling in for David these past weeks but he hadn't created any problems. Perhaps someone was ill.

His sleek Jaguar sped toward the family estate. This was unusual. Dependable David, his older brother, kept everything under control, never any surprises. He was due back any day now. Had something happened to him?

Andrew's black car swished through rain-slicked streets and he scowled, expecting the worst. What if it was only his matchmaking mother with another witless wonder she thought would make him a good wife? No . . . his mother wouldn't sound distressed over some hopeful marriage prospect; anyway, she knew marriage wasn't on his agenda.

His mother wished he'd settle down, but at thirty-four, Andrew felt no need for a wife. Sure, women were only too willing to spend his money, but what was in a marriage for him? He screeched to a halt, almost running through a red light, then drummed his fingers on the steering wheel, asking himself what he wanted in a marriage partner.

He wanted an independent woman, someone with a life of her own, strong enough to talk back, someone to share ideas with, someone who loved art, music, and sailing. He shook his head as the light changed. That was too much to ask from one woman. He'd stay single.

As he turned onto a tree-lined street, he thought of David, only four years older but already graying at the temples and developing a paunch. To David, making money was everything. He saw timber rights, feet of lumber and market potential, never the beauty of the forest. He never smelled the tang of greenery or heard the rustle of wind in the branches.

Andrew hiked the wilderness trails and stared in awe at the old-growth forest. Not expected to take over the Tracklin Empire as David was, he could study forestry for the sheer joy of it.

His sleek car slipped through the iron gates, up the driveway lit by lamps concealed in the shrubbery, and stopped abruptly in front of the stately mansion.

Two large barking dogs bounded out, alerting Mrs. Wilson, the housekeeper, 'her wee boy Andy' had arrived— and not a moment too soon.

Andrew hugged the elderly woman but was given no chance to speak. "Thank heavens you've come. Your parents are fit to be tied." She paused, taking in Andrew's questioning gaze. "There's been some news."

"Where are they?"

"In the sitting room. I warn you . . . they're in a temper." She turned toward the kitchen. "I'll send up tea."

The yellow room, verdant with green plants, looked cheery, but the two occupants were anything but. Rebecca Tracklin, her face drained of color, sat in her favorite armchair, in hushed conversation with her agitated husband.

At the sight of her son, the deep lines of stress eased and she rose to embrace him.

"What's going on? Why the gloomy faces? Has there been a death?"

Andrew's eyes traveled to his father, who stopped his pacing and stood behind his wife's chair. His face was flushed with barely-controlled fury, his fists were tightly clenched at his sides. He ground his teeth in anger but made no attempt to explain.

Mrs. Tracklin answered quietly, "No dear, there's been no death." She paused, searching for the appropriate words, the look on her face bleak. "Something unexpected . . . we weren't prepared . . ." She took a deep breath. Her blue eyes, the same color as her son's, begged for understanding, words seemed choked in her throat.

Then it came. "Your brother David has married!"

Robert Tracklin cursed under his breath, "Damn fool!"

"Married? David?" Andrew grinned. "When? Who's the girl?"

His mother's severe look gave warning; this wasn't a laughing matter. His father, rigid and scowling, seethed fury. Some woman had disrupted his plans for David.

"Damn floozy. That's who."

"We only know her name is Monique and they were married three days ago."

"Should never have sent him to Montreal. No good came of it." Anger glittered in Robert Tracklin's fevered eyes. "Some French Canadian singer got her claws into him. Now he's going to abandon all I've built." He shook his fist to punctuate his words. Then his shoulders slumped, his gray head bowed and he looked as if all life had drained from his frail body.

Andrew put a consoling arm around his father's shoulders. "Don't be hard on David. He's dedicated to Tracklin's, worked long hours without complaint; now doesn't he deserve to choose his own wife?"

"It's a disgrace! Can't have known her more than a week."

"Love at first sight, Father. Don't you believe it can happen?"

The low growl made Andrew change his tactics. He'd appeal to his father's rational side. He knew well his father's unforgiving anger and pride. He could sympathize with his brother, the pressure he had been under all these years.

"David isn't impulsive. He's methodical. Nothing distracts him from business. You can depend on his choices." Andrew paused, letting his reasonable argument sink in. Then he added with emphasis, "Monique must be one special woman!"

Robert Tracklin was not convinced.

"Opportunist. That what she is! After his money."

He condemned his new daughter-in-law before meeting her.

"Give them a chance. David's happiness is worth more than all the money Tracklin's can make."

Scowling, bloodless lips pressed together, Robert Tracklin gave a withering look to the only man who dared challenge him. Unwilling to admit it, he couldn't deny his son's point. He'd been strict with David, expected him to be responsible, take over the family business. It was true; he'd had little chance to make his own choices.

"What's gotten into David? It's a waste!"

"He's in love, Father."

Andrew hoped a daughter-in-law would cheer his parents. But if Robert Tracklin was happily contemplating grandchildren, there was no sign of it. He gritted his teeth, eyes flaring, filled with angry frustration.

Rebecca Tracklin's quiet voice injected calm into the tension crackling between father and son. "Your father worries about the pulp mill and lumber contracts on Desolation Sound. David was in charge, but if he doesn't return from Montreal as planned, the deal is left hanging. Many jobs depend on that mill."

Her voice drifted off but her son heard the plea for help. His father had a heart condition and all this stress was not good for him. Andrew read the concern in his mother's gentle face.

His father's features were lined from exhaustion, eyes puffy, deep creases scoring his cheeks—a proud man who asked favors of no one. He trusted his eldest son to carry on the family tradition but now the future of Tracklin's was in doubt. All he had worked for his whole life was in danger of being destroyed. His youngest son was capable, but was he willing to accept the responsibility for more than a few weeks?

He eyed the slender young man whose tanned face

showed none of the strain so characteristic of David; his alert blue eyes sparkled with humor, another trait lacking in his eldest son. The proud man swallowed with difficulty, choking back words he didn't want to utter. He lifted beseeching eyes.

"Andrew, will you take over David's position in the company?"

Not convinced David had thrown it all over for good, and concerned about his father's health, Andrew nodded. He could play lumber baron for a few more months . . . until David sorted things out.

"I'll do it . . . as a wedding present to the happy couple."

His father gagged. "If it lasts!"

He studied his youngest son who lacked David's seriousness. "It involves tree planting, running the mill, and plans to spray parts of the standing timber." This dour information given, he added gruffly, "Just stick to business, son, and you'll do fine."

As visions of the curly-haired woman on the hillside danced before his eyes, Andrew's deep laughter met his father's strict orders. "What else could I stick to in a place called Desolation Sound?"

Chapter Two

Footsteps clomped toward the Corwins' kitchen door. All heads turned as Daniel staggered in, his sandy hair disheveled, his face spattered with mud. Vengeance burned in his eyes.

Julie gasped.

"What's happened?"

He rolled his eyes, rubbed his arm where his shirt was torn, but said nothing.

"Geraldine get you again, Dad?" Jake's voice hinted laughter not sympathy.

"Drat that goat! She hates me." His face softened at the sight of his laughing family. It was a joy to see them smiling and relaxed after the past difficult weeks.

He spread his arms and grinned. "Look at me—bullfighters come out better than this."

Life settled into a pleasant routine on Desolation Sound. Anna's spirits lifted, and with her instructions Julie was able to run the household. Her creative cooking and cheerful nature were welcome additions after Anna's frightening accident. She was the only one they could turn to when they needed help so desperately. The family was thriving and Daniel was confident he could leave them for ten days to go tree planting.

Glad she hadn't told Anna about her planned trip to Hawaii, Julie treasured this time spent with her sister, surprised to find she enjoyed the chores of simple living.

This was quite a change from the three-month vacation she had arranged with the travel agent. Those glossy travel brochures still sat on the coffee table in her west end condo. Instead of sunshine, palm trees and tropical flowers, she was enjoying foggy mist, cold sea breeze and a vegetable garden that took constant work. She wasn't wearing flimsy beach outfits and lying in the sun; she wore tattered work clothes and was on her feet from dawn till dusk.

She wouldn't trade these past weeks for any sun-drenched paradise.

Anna watched her sister with that far-away look. Her first day on Desolation Sound, Julie looked like she'd stepped from a fashion magazine—styled hair, tapered nails, elegantly dressed. But look at her now—a messy sprite in overalls, unruly curls, and fingernails dirty from the garden. She felt a tightness in her throat, swamped by a wave of gratitude. She knew the comforts Julie had given up to be here; not many sisters would make such a sacrifice, and without a word of complaint.

She knew of Julie's luxury condo in Vancouver, her success at Northern Chemicals, and the sophisticated city life she was used to.

Anna's eyes grew misty, she had never loved or needed her sister more. And Julie hadn't let her down.

This rustic setting couldn't be easy for her—no convenient grocery store, no hot showers, no television, or friends close enough to visit. She watched Julie push another piece of wood into the cook stove. She saw the little girl with a flair for make-believe all grown up but still having that enthusiasm for life. She never imagined her little sister would be looking after her—but here she was, and making it look like she enjoyed every second.

Daniel interrupted her thoughts.

He was fidgeting about; something was on his mind. His gentle voice told all.

"Someone has to milk Geraldine while I'm gone."

Silence.

Julie looked around the kitchen table. There were no volunteers. Daniel nodded when the light dawned and she raised disbelieving eyes to his bearded face.

She looked to Anna, her arm and leg in casts. She couldn't milk the goat in her condition.

Anna's eyes twinkled. "It's not so hard, Julie. Keep talking to Geraldine . . . sometimes singing helps."

"Sing? Me? That goat isn't deaf. And you know how off-key I sing."

"She's a little creature . . . truly gentle at heart." Julie's wide-eyed stare told her sister she didn't believe a word of it. She'd seen that goat butting the gate and chewing sheets as they hung on the clothesline. That goat was a menace.

Anna leaned forward and lowered her voice. "Without her we're stuck with powdered milk."

A chorus of groans followed the words 'powdered milk.'

Beyond the window, the gray-green sea lapped against the rocky shore, the setting sun colored the clouds pink and mauve as seagulls glided in lazy patterns. The undisturbed calm buoyed Julie's spirit.

She surrendered. How hard could milking a goat be? She was a chemical engineer. She'd handled worse things than this.

"Okay, I'll do it. Tomorrow morning, I milk Geraldine."

The distant noise of a helicopter fueled Julie's determination. No bad-tempered goat and no blue-eyed pilot were going to disrupt the life Anna and Daniel had worked so hard to build.

* * *

As she drifted into sleep, Julie grappled with the problem of milking the goat, but no foolproof strategy formed in her mind. Instead, the handsome face of the pilot kept appearing, distracting her and haunting her dreams. This isolation must be getting to her.

Next morning, when she sat down on the milking stool beside Geraldine, she half expected to see the face of that Tracklin man peering back at her. Reassuring for her sanity, it was a goat face returning her glance.

"Speak soothingly," Anna had said.

"Well, here we are alone together, Geraldine," Julie soothed, setting her feet firmly on the ground as she settled her bottom onto the stool. "We need your milk. Stand still, that's a good girl; keep all four feet on the ground."

The curious animal turned slanting eyes on Julie. She didn't move, but the yellow glow in her eyes made Julie nervous. She kept talking, as much to soothe herself as the goat.

"You're a lovely goat, Geraldine, soulful eyes, stringy fur, spindly legs." The goat remained motionless, only her tail twitching. Julie dared to reach out a tentative hand.

Instantly, Geraldine lowered her head, then struck out with her hind leg, kicking Julie full in the chest.

Julie had the breath knocked out of her, but with the pillow tied inside her overalls taking the worst of the blow, she kept from toppling backward. She wasn't pleased but she kept her voice soft and soothing.

"That wasn't nice, Geraldine."

This time the unpredictable goat allowed Julie to make contact. Her tail swished threateningly but Julie kept talking and a stream of milk began to cover the bottom of the empty pail.

Heartened by her success, Julie hummed a lullaby vaguely remembered from her youth. The milk flowed faster, Geraldine stopped fidgeting, and Julie released the breath she'd been holding.

"Good girl," she whispered. "We'll try this again to-morrow."

The ornery goat bleated, anxious to get free.

She led Geraldine back to pasture, where the goat frisked across the rough ground, stretching her legs, daring anyone to try and catch her. Julie carefully carried the pail to the house. Her bulky padding made walking awkward, but cheers met her at the door when she displayed the goat's milk.

For a girl she was pretty brave, Jake thought. He'd never in a million years attempt to milk that mean goat. Julie was alright.

"Our precious jewel," said Anna.

"What's that, Mommy . . . a precious jool?"

"Something very dear."

Simon turned the words over on his tongue, his dark eyes sparkling. "I like that," he concluded in his three-year-old wisdom.

That afternoon, as Simon napped and Julie massaged the stiffness out of Anna's shoulder where the heavy plaster cast made her muscles ache, the two sisters talked, sharing everything as they had as children.

"Have you seen Ian Sutherland?"

"Only once . . . at a retirement dinner for Dr. Webb. He looked down his nose at me and said my red dress wasn't proper. Respectable women don't wear red."

"The nerve! Bright colors suit you." Anna was indignant in her sister's defense. "Was he always so critical?"

"I didn't notice at first. He was the older engineer to my struggling student. I thought it was friendly advice."

"Hmph!" Anna scoffed. "I remember you trying so hard to please him. It worried me."

"I was too blind to be warned." Julie imitated Ian's critical voice. "He didn't like my clothes. He didn't like my hair. My friends were too noisy. Before I woke up, I was trying to be someone I didn't like just to get his approval."

Anna shook her head. "And then there was his mother."

"Oh, don't forget her! 'A woman doesn't need a career,' she said. 'A proper wife stays at home to look after her husband and children.' " Julie shrugged her shoulders, then adjusted the sling and continued to massage Anna's other shoulder.

"What did Ian think?"

"He agreed . . . now that I look back, I see how I tried to make myself over."

"What made you see the light?"

"One day I was trying on a new dress. I looked at myself in the shop mirror and was astounded. It was something Ian's mother would choose. What a shock! I was about to buy the dress but I didn't like it at all. That jostled me awake. My eyes were open then!"

"You could never have been happy with Ian. He'd only get worse."

Julie stopped to stare at her quiet-spoken sister. "Listen to you—old wise woman of the west! How did you get so smart?"

Anna grinned. "I was always the smart one."

"Ha! Modest too!"

They laughed as Julie shifted to the floor and removed the wool sock, leaving Anna's bare foot sticking out of her cast. The cold toes were colorless, but rubbing them between her warm hands began to bring the circulation back.

"You were right. He tried to take over my life." Julie paused. "Are any men comfortable with career women? Ian wasn't pleased when I started at Northern Chemicals. He accused me of being married to my job and said no man would want me."

"Nonsense! He was jealous."

"I wanted to celebrate my success but he could only criticize. He couldn't understand how exciting chemistry is to me."

Anna didn't share that excitement, either, but she knew how important it was to Julie and was happy for her. "Just wait . . . one day some man will arouse chemistry in you more exciting than anything in that lab of yours."

"Dream on," Julie moaned.

Anna reached out her one good arm to hug her sister. "Believe me, the right man is out there. You're too good for the likes of Ian Sutherland."

"Wiggle your toes," Julie instructed. "Keep moving them, keep the circulation going in your foot." Anna obeyed.

Julie sighed. "I don't believe in miracles."

"It will happen . . . call it chemistry . . . your feelings will take over and that will be that."

"I'm short on trust after the way Ian turned on me. You and Daniel never had any doubts from the very day you met—relationships like yours are rare."

Julie seldom argued with her sister, but on this they differed. Only in her dreams did men encourage her independence. She knew Anna didn't agree . . . so she quickly changed the subject.

"Speaking of feelings, I had a strange experience that day the children and I picked bramble berries."

"Tell me more."

"When that helicopter pilot started to move toward us, the sun behind him, it was as though the sun went behind a cloud. I was chilled to the bone."

"But it was a hot, sunny day."

"I know. He appeared so large and menacing."

"That doesn't sound like you. Did he say anything to make you mad?"

"No, he just swaggered across the field as if he owned the place."

"Someone from Tracklin's?"

Julie nodded. "Who else flies over this hill?"

Anna smiled, her hazel-green eyes sparkling. "Maybe it was Prince Charming."

"Ha! More likely the giant from under the sea!"

The two sisters laughed.

"You always were afraid of giants, never witches or ghosts . . . only giants."

Julie nodded. But that Tracklin man was nothing like the ugly giants of her childhood nightmares. They never were lean and fit with blond hair, blue eyes and a blinding smile. And they didn't come in helicopters.

She was saved from anymore of her sister's interrogation by Simon, who woke from his nap and wanted something to eat.

Anna got in the last teasing comment. "Girl, you over-reacted. That's a sign."

Julie glared back at her sister over the sandwich makings she had pulled out for Simon. The unspoken question, "A sign of what?" hung in the air between them.

That evening, as she walked along the rocky shoreline to give the Corwins some precious time alone together, Julie turned Anna's words over in her mind.

A slight breeze off the water ruffled her hair; the sea was calm, the distant small islands casting dark shadows in the blue-green ocean. She inhaled deeply, feeling the cool air fill her lungs, releasing with it the tension of worry over Anna's recovery. Her reaction to that Tracklin man seemed distant and unimportant as the gentle lapping of waves and the smell of salt air soothed her.

Captain Cook must have found this a lonely place to name it Desolation Sound, but its peaceful serenity and natural beauty were a remedy after her hectic city life.

So many thoughts were crowding her mind; loneliness and desolation were not among them.

Anna said 'your feelings take over.' She meant romantic

feelings like she had for Daniel, but no man overpowered Julie with wild feelings; she was a scientist, reason and logic won out.

She turned back to reach the Corwin house before darkness fell.

Feelings that take over, she mused. She was too sensible for that. A scientist needed hard facts, not sentimental imaginings.

That helicopter pilot aroused feelings . . . but that wasn't romantic . . . that was something else . . . suspicion and distrust. Perhaps Anna was right, she was overreacting. Her concerns about protecting the forest and saving the environment were misplaced here, in this untouched wilderness.

All the same, she was thankful she wasn't going to see that Tracklin man again.

Daniel wondered about the warm welcome Bruce Sorkin gave him when he joined the planting crew. Few returned for a season of back-breaking stooping and heavy slogging over rough ground to tamp tiny seedlings into the logged hillside. But that didn't explain Bruce's unusual interest in Anna and the children.

Suspicious of Bruce? Daniel shook his head. *I've been isolated too long,* he thought as he packed his gear for the grueling ten-day excursion.

On the second day, the Tracklin helicopter flew low over the planting area. *Must be some change in our instructions,* Daniel reasoned. But when Bruce Sorkin's gray head appeared amidst the crew for lunch, no mention of changes was made.

As Daniel hoisted his backpack to return to work, Bruce called to him. "Walk back to the helicopter with me, the new boss asked to meet you."

To Daniel's puzzled look he replied, "Seems he saw your family picking berries . . . was curious."

Andrew Tracklin, deep in conversation with a member

of the logging crew, noticed the two men approaching. "Ready, Bruce? The slash burning problem is settled— we'll truck out the big chunks, leave the rest to compost and eliminate smoke hanging over the valley."

Bruce nodded silent agreement then turned to Daniel. "Andrew Tracklin, this is Daniel Corwin. He has a place on Desolation Sound."

Inquisitive eyes studied Daniel's bearded face and the quiet way he carried himself. "Pleased to meet you," Mr. Tracklin said as he shook hands. "I've already had the pleasure of meeting your family."

Daniel was surprised by the claim but said nothing, curious why the head of Tracklin's was making small talk with a tree planter.

Andrew was equally curious, wondering how this quiet philosopher and the vivacious woman he met on the hillside had ever married. *No wonder he comes on the planting crew, to get a break from his wife. A man could be driven to distraction by a woman like that, removed from the luxuries of civilization, constantly in each other's company.*

He gave voice to none of these thoughts, merely saying, "I hope your family is well."

Daniel smiled, calmly taking in the intense stare fixed on his face and the feeling of expectation, waiting for him to answer.

"They're fine."

A man of few words, thought Andrew, but he didn't turn away or focus his attention elsewhere, encouraging Daniel to elaborate.

"I'm worried about getting my wife to the doctor in Powell River next week. The boat trip is rough if the weather doesn't hold."

Andrew raised both eyebrows. "Something serious?"

"She slipped and fell onto rocks, broke her arm and leg. She's ready to have her casts removed."

The memory of dark eyes flashing on that sunny hillside

softened the lines around Andrew's eyes. "I could help. I fly the planting crew out next week; I could deliver you home, then fly you and your wife to Powell River. It's only a few minutes by air . . . might save a lot of discomfort."

Daniel smiled, genuinely grateful. "That's kind of you."

"The least I can do for a neighbor." He gestured to Bruce to buckle up and slipped into the pilot's seat.

Daniel resumed planting where he'd left off and the Tracklin helicopter lifted directly into the air and disappeared.

"Looks like you'll get the chance," Bruce grinned, "to ask the one woman who didn't swoon at your feet, what she found so objectionable?"

A wry grin turned up the corners of Andrew Tracklin's mouth, his eyes hidden behind dark glasses. "Watch your mouth, Sorkin," he warned. "It's a long drop to the ground."

Bruce laughed. He'd never seen the boss touchy before, certainly not over a woman.

As Daniel paced methodically across the bald hillside, bending, chopping a hole, firming in the seedling, then resuming his pace, his thoughts returned to Andrew Tracklin saying he'd met his family. It couldn't have been Anna, it was Julie he saw picking berries. *Why didn't I think of that before? Oh well, I don't suppose it makes much difference.*

Friday morning dawned clear with a brisk wind from the north, making Julie uneasy about rough seas and her sister's trip to the doctor. She dissolved yeast in warm water and began making bread, anticipating Daniel's return. When the children sat down to breakfast, the kitchen was warm, yeasty-smelling from the rising bread dough and tingling with excitement.

"Schoolwork is canceled today," Julie announced. "Your mom needs her hair washed and your dad is due home. Let's celebrate—your mom's casts are coming off."

"Good," Simon sighed. "I haven't had a two-arm hug in ages."

Jake and Moira laughed at their little brother while Julie dippered hot water from the reservoir beside the wood stove, ready to shampoo her sister's long black hair.

"This is luxury," Anna sighed. "I could get used to having a hairdresser in residence. Do you remember how you hated hair washing when you were a little girl?"

"I hated having the knots brushed out."

"I still can see the horrified look on Mother's face when you took the scissors and gave yourself a haircut." The two sisters laughed. One sister had been so serene and accepting, the other mischievous and challenging.

"Mother told me I should try to be sensible, like you."

Picking up a note of sadness, Anna assured her sister, "In her way, she loved you, Julie. She was proud that you were independent and incorrigible. She felt apologetic about her meekness."

Never as close to her mother as her sister, Julie nodded. "I suppose you're right." She recalled the past. "She was never able to understand or encourage me. She thought I should marry and raise a family; not go to university. She told me, 'No one wants an educated woman.' "

Julie paused with that cold criticism echoing in her mind. "Come to think of it, Ian said exactly that too."

Dripping water from her towel-dried hair, Anna put her arm around her sister. "She'd be proud of you if she were alive today. In her time, it was rare for a woman to be independent and successful, she couldn't imagine it. She didn't easily express her feelings, but she loved you Julie. Believe me, she wanted the best for you."

With Anna sitting by the stove drying her long hair, Julie cast anxious glances at the angry sea churning up high waves outside. It reflected the darkness of the clouds, no longer blue-green in color, now an ominous slate gray. She could hear gulls scree as they flew inland, and hear the wind swooshing down the chimney causing small puffs of smoke to escape the burning wood stove. There would be sad faces this evening if a storm built and Daniel was unable to make it home.

As she removed four loaves of perfectly baked bread from the oven, added more wood to maintain the heat, then pushed the bread buns in, the clatter of helicopter blades set her nerves on edge. The wind must be carrying the sound, making it louder than usual, so loud it could be right in Geraldine's pasture.

Moira, who had been in the hen house gathering eggs, put her basket on the table and dashed back out the door. "It's Daddy!" she squealed as she ran to catch up with her brothers.

Anna smoothed her drying hair out of her face. "Is it true? Has Daniel been flown home?" A worried frown marred her pretty face. "Is he hurt?"

Watching from the window, Julie saw Daniel step from the helicopter with outstretched arms that enfolded three ecstatic children. "It's true, Anna. And no, he's not hurt. The children are on top of him but he's not hurt."

"Help me to the window, I want to see for myself."

This done, Julie turned to remove the loaves of bread from their pans and set them to cool while Anna watched the events in the pasture.

"Who's brought Daniel home? Look, he's coming to the house, not returning to camp."

Joining Anna at the window, Julie's eyes grew large. Even through darkened sky and brisk wind, she recognized that figure. "Him!"

With his sun-streaked hair mussed by removing his helmet, the pilot smiled at the children welcoming their father home. The wind molded trousers against his well-muscled thighs, topped by a white, cable-knit sweater that accentuated the tan on his handsome face. He walked with the grace of an athlete, not bothered by the wind or threat of rain, Simon bouncing on his shoulders.

Thunderclouds gathered in Julie's eyes, her heart beat rapidly, and her body tensed. I hadn't expected to see that man again. Now would be a good time for Geraldine to kick someone, but look at that silly goat, chewing the grass at the edge of the vegetable garden, not even lifting her head.

Daniel reached the doorway first, rushed to Anna, held her slender face in his hands and kissed her tenderly for what seemed a very long time.

The pilot stood in the doorway taking in the scene, without expression. Nothing on his face or in his stance hinted at the thoughts racing through his mind. He lowered Simon to the ground, his gaze focused on Julie's backside as she bent over the oven door removing freshly baked bread buns. No one could have suspected the word 'bigamy' was flashing before him; his self-control was remarkable. He remained calmly by the door betraying none of his reactions, as though every day he encountered a man with two wives. *No wonder he'd chosen this isolated setting. No neighbors to ask questions.*

His large frame filled the doorway. Julie hadn't expected to see him here in the Corwins' house. The life of a corporate executive didn't usually include visits to remote homesteads.

Ever the polite host, Daniel made the introductions. "Mr. Tracklin, this is my wife, Anna." Then he gestured toward Julie. "And I believe you've already met my sister-in-law, Julie."

An inscrutable smile lit his face, his body relaxed, and Julie noticed the suspicious way he'd been looking at them vanished. "Yes," he intoned in his deep voice. "We crossed paths in a berry patch."

There was something suggestive about the way he said that.

"So we did, Mr. Tracklin, an unlogged berry patch in pristine wilderness." There was no doubt she was criticizing the lumber company's presence here but Julie hadn't time to elaborate.

Daniel was telling Anna, "Mr. Tracklin has offered to fly us to Powell River. How soon can you be ready?"

"I'm ready now . . . if you get my shawl and crutches."

Andrew Tracklin grinned. *Daniel's sister-in-law had spark. He'd give her that.* He was trying to piece together her presence there. Never one to make sense of second cousins, in-laws and aunts-twice-removed, he was searching his brain, although his cool composure gave no evidence of it.

It occurred to him that Monique was his sister-in-law, his brother's wife, so that must make the curly-haired beauty Daniel's brother's wife.

That settled to his satisfaction, he scanned the spacious room that served as kitchen, living room and dining room, inhaling the heavenly aroma of baked bread, noting the filled wood box beside the stove, the pail of water carried up from a well, and the absence of microwave, refrigerator or television. She must have plenty of experience with this sort of living, no woman he knew could nurse an invalid, tend three children, run a homestead and look like she had energy left to burn.

But if she was married, where was her husband? Could she be Daniel's sister-in-law and not be married to his brother? He looked closely . . . she wasn't wearing a wedding ring. *Maybe she took it off for doing chores.* He couldn't just blurt out and ask, "Are you married?"

Here on familiar ground, Julie wasn't threatened by the tall expanse of man looking out of place with his cultivated good looks in this simple setting.

Still, something about the man was intimidating. He was studying her like a specimen under glass. Her past over-reaction was an embarrassment, but she faced him boldly. "Could I offer you a cup of tea, Mr. Tracklin?"

She caught him off guard. "No . . . thank you," he managed. "But I would enjoy a glass of cold water."

Julie dippered it from the water pail and handed it to their guest, her flashing brown eyes daring him to ask for an ice cube, something unheard of in this house.

He registered the dare in her eyes but didn't give her the satisfaction of responding. If he was amused or insulted, he didn't let on. "Thank you," he said politely.

He had gathered Julie was here to help the Corwins during Anna's convalescence. His curiosity got the better of him. "Do you and your husband live nearby?"

Julie had turned to help Anna, but Moira heard, and giggled. "Julie doesn't have a husband. She lives far away." She looked up at the tall man so sweetly but she had no idea she had provided the very information he wanted to know.

Bending to pull thick socks onto Anna's bare feet, Julie was taken aback by her sister's troubled face. She had been so long-suffering and never a word of complaint. Now that she was to be spared the uncomfortable boat trip, what could be making her frown so? She was shaking. The room was hot from the stove, so she couldn't be cold.

Anna attempted a wobbly smile but Julie wasn't convinced. The fear in her eyes gave her away. Julie gave her a silent questioning look.

"I'm worried about flying," she whispered.

This was Anna, who had crewed on the most flimsy sailboats in raging seas with never a qualm, fearful about flying.

Julie grinned. "You'll do fine." She squeezed Anna's hand. "Keep thinking what's ahead—an arm that bends and a leg to stand on." She tied her sister's shoe and helped her upright. "It'll be worth a few minutes in the air."

Anna was repeating these words to herself like a charm

to ward off disaster, "An arm that bends, a leg to stand on," when her husband picked her up and carried her to the door. The fierce wind caught Anna's shawl and swept it across Daniel's face. Julie brushed it aside and reached up to tuck it tightly around her sister.

Her attentions to Anna hadn't gone unnoticed. Andrew watched her carrying crutches and a basket to the helicopter, strong and sure-footed as she climbed the rocky incline. He trailed behind with the children. All this fresh air and exercise must account for the beautiful vitality he'd never noticed in other women. The cold sea air and swirling wind had no effect on her.

Tucking the picnic hamper into the helicopter, Julie kissed her sister gently on the cheek, her eyes catching the pilot's as he slipped behind the controls. She didn't lower her head, but stared boldly, her curly hair tossed about in wild array by the increasing wind. He seemed to swallow her with his eyes, trying to balance the touching family scene with the hostile reception he'd encountered on the hillside.

As Anna nervously braced for takeoff, Julie's eyes softened, grateful Anna was spared that boat trip in windy seas.

"Thank you for flying Anna to Powell River, Mr. Tracklin." Her quiet voice had a melodic quality he remembered. "We appreciate your kindness."

Taken by surprise, he nodded acknowledgment. He hadn't expected sweet gratitude from the elusive woman. Checking his controls, he felt off-balance, an unfamiliar state for a nerveless pilot. "My pleasure," he said softly.

This woman didn't behave as expected. She wasn't impressed by his association with Tracklin's. Briskly, he donned his helmet and dark glasses and gestured everyone to move clear of the blades.

The helicopter lifted off; Julie and the children waved from the middle of the field but Anna saw none of it. Daniel held her hand but her eyes remained firmly shut.

The pilot's attention was drawn down into the clearing. Wild, dark curls were being tossed about in the wind and soft feminine curves were visible even through a baggy shirt and ragged blue jeans. What an intense creature she was, first suspicious and hostile, then sincerely grateful. For a moment there, she seemed almost vulnerable. He couldn't deny . . . he was intrigued.

He swung his eyes up from the pasture as the first raindrops began to fall. *She's not married,* he told himself— *but she's out of bounds. I'm only here for a short time. It wouldn't do to get involved with someone I have no chance of seeing again.*

He focused on flying the Corwins to hospital as quickly and smoothly as possible.

Yet, Julie's flashing eyes and apparent disinterest presented a challenge he couldn't get out of his mind.

Chapter Three

That afternoon passed in a whirlwind of activity, whipping laundry off the outdoor clothesline and hanging it inside to dry, sweeping floors, tidying the house and making preparations for dinner. Through it all, Julie was haunted by clear blue eyes that looked right through her as if she was transparent. She had no defense, not even Geraldine was on her side.

That man's air of authority brought up warning signals. Ian had been like that and she hadn't fared well with him.

Mr. Tracklin enjoyed wealth and power, landed wherever he pleased, disrupted the lives of ordinary people, and left her feeling uneasy. Daniel told her Tracklin's planned to modernize the pulp mill, putting men out of work. That man had a ruthless streak and could be dangerous. She'd be wise to stay out of his way, not aggravate the situation; she was only here a little while longer.

Moira, so like her mother, glowed with a quiet excitement as she inspected the polished house, fresh flowers on the table, and a lovely cake cooling beside the stove. "Mommy will be happy."

The early morning wind died down as quickly as it had come up, replaced by a stillness in the woods, not a leaf rustling or a branch swaying. Julie crossed her fingers hoping Anna's first flight went smoothly. It was funny her sister, usually so very brave, had one small weakness when it came to flying, a weakness no one had suspected before today.

She dismissed the thought, headed for the vegetable garden and went in through the gate in the fence that kept deer from eating the plants she'd nurtured so carefully these past six weeks. With a pitchfork, she dug a hill of new potatoes for dinner; Moira picked leafy lettuce, and Jake and Simon gathered the first ripe strawberries.

The water was icy as she pumped it over the little potatoes, washing off the clinging bits of dirt. An ever-increasing sound approached and she didn't have to look up to know what was heading for the clearing. That Tracklin man was back.

The sight of Anna holding up two arms banished Julie's irritation. She rushed to the helicopter with the children, her jeans wet and clinging where water splattered on them at the pump, her shirt sleeves rolled up, and her hair tied back with a piece of string.

Anna's pleasure, free of cumbersome casts, glowed on her face. "What a relief! The doctor said I'm healing well but I have exercises to do to regain my strength."

Daniel, a man of few words, was beaming. He was worried about Anna's recovery but never let on. They would be unable to remain on Desolation Sound if Anna's good health and boundless energy didn't return. The crisis was over.

With her children carefully hugging her and extolling the wonderful dinner being prepared, Anna sighed. She loved this spot on Desolation Sound. It was her piece of heaven. Nothing could make her leave—not backbreaking work, long wet winters, and certainly not broken limbs.

She turned to look the pilot full in the face where he sat behind the controls watching the homecoming, her joy and contentment unmistakable. "Join us for dinner, Mr. Track-lin. We have little to repay you—our fare may be humble but it's shared gladly."

Only a man of stone could refuse such heart-warming hospitality.

"I'd be honored." His eyes flicked to Julie in hesitation. "That is, if it's no inconvenience."

"Good heavens, no," Anna's gentle voice brushed aside any chance of his refusal. "You're as welcome as the flowers in spring."

Julie swallowed hard, trying not to choke. Sometimes Anna was too sweet-tempered to be believed. And to top it off, that Tracklin man threw a smug grin in Julie's direction, fully aware of her unvoiced objections.

He stepped out of the helicopter and sauntered over, so tall he towered a full foot above her. His clothing wasn't even rumpled and neither was his self-assurance.

She tipped back her head to look up into those cool blue eyes. "We can always use an extra pair of hands." She pointed to the water pump. "If you could carry those vegetables to the house . . ." Muttering to herself, she mimicked his own words and tone of voice so quietly she was sure no one could hear, "That is, if it's no inconvenience."

He heard, biting his cheek to keep from grinning. Obediently, he walked across the pasture to the water pump and picked up the washed potatoes and lettuce, still shedding droplets of cold water.

For a moment, before carrying Anna's bag and the picnic basket back to the house, Julie stared at the back and broad shoulders of the man moving with long strides and fluid grace. He hadn't said much but he was infuriating!

Long before Anna had hobbled across the uneven ground with Daniel's help, Mr. Tracklin delivered the required vegetables to the kitchen. Julie was drizzling the salmon with lemon juice and adding sprigs of dill before putting it in the oven.

"That looks delicious," he said sincerely. "Are you a professional chef?"

Julie laughed. "Far from it!" She thought of her lab work and the chemical reactions she dealt with, then laughed again at the idea of anyone thinking she was a professional chef.

She accepted the garden produce, put the potatoes on to steam, then began savagely tearing lettuce for a salad.

Thankfully, Jake and Moira dragged Mr. Tracklin off by the hand to show him their schoolwork before she had to make further conversation with the suave man who probably saw this labor-intensive lifestyle as primitive.

Had she but known, he was impressed with their resourcefulness. He welcomed the children bustling around him, hesitant to be alone with Julie. He wouldn't admit it, but she unnerved him, made him incoherent the instant she turned those accusing dark brown eyes on him. Just what she was accusing him of, he had no idea. It was obvious she objected to his presence here . . . and that bothered him.

He was also impressed with the children's work; isolation hadn't affected their education. In fact, Jake and Moira were more poised and knowledgeable than most children their ages and were delighted to have an attentive visitor to share things with.

When Anna finally made it to the house, Julie settled her in an armchair, puffed a cushion and placed it behind her back, then raised her right ankle on a footstool—so natural and caring, with no trace of resentment or impatience. He admired her unselfish attention. She lifted her head to study Anna's tired face but instead, looked up into a handsome male face, watching her closely, taking in every move.

He didn't look away, unrepentant at being caught staring. Not many women put another person's needs ahead of their own. He couldn't disguise his curiosity. Their eyes met briefly, like a clash of swords, steely blue meeting flashing brown with sparks flying but neither one willing to retreat.

Andrew smiled. "You do that very well. Are you a trained nurse?"

Julie shook her head. "I'd be a dreadful nurse; I haven't the patience."

Daniel interrupted, holding a package wrapped in brown paper. "I picked up our mail this afternoon. This is for you, Julie."

She recognized the handwriting and smiled.

From across the room, Andrew watched as she removed the paper from a purple candy box—Purdy's, he noted. Whoever sent her candy spared no expense. She looked pleased but not all that impressed. He wondered why. She couldn't receive gifts often way out here at the back of beyond.

A letter from the project manager accompanied the box, telling her the latest happenings at Northern Chemicals and wishing her well.

"Who's it from?"

"Martin. Knowing my chocolate cravings, he figured I must be unbearable by now." She lifted the lid and admired the candy in fluted black papers, inhaling the tempting scent of dark chocolate.

Anna knew her sister; chocolate was a weakness. She raised her finger. "No sweets till after supper. They'll keep."

"Oh, Anna. Just one?"

She laughed. Her little sister hadn't changed. She may be a clever engineer, but that impetuous child was still there underneath. "Not even one." She tried to sound severe but her smiling eyes gave her away.

Julie replaced the lid. "You always were the sensible one."

Mr. Tracklin was taking all this in with undisguised interest. Julie shrugged her shoulders and stared back, just daring him to make some sarcastic remark, but he said nothing, merely noted her belligerent look and held back his amusement. She must have been a handful as a child.

She turned her attention to the stove. Supper was ready, the salmon fragrant with dill and the vegetables cooked to perfection. With Simon setting out plates, Moira adding cutlery, and Jake glasses, the table was quickly set.

Julie couldn't ignore Andrew; he seemed to enjoy her discomfort. She looked at him and ordered, "The serving dishes still need to be filled."

Daniel and Anna exchanged glances at Julie's tone. It was so unlike her to snap at people. She wasn't like her usual self around their guest; he had rattled her nerves.

Mr. Tracklin did as instructed, aware of the dark eyes watching him. He casually stood beside her, basking in the heat radiating from the wood fire, filling the dishes she handed him from the pots on the stove, close enough for her to be aware of his great height and the elusive fragrance of a masculine cologne.

She sensed, in spite of acting like a docile kitchen maid, he was fully in control, ready to assert his strength whenever it suited him.

She looked around at the familiar surroundings, Daniel helping Anna to the table, the children taking their places, the glow of evening light reflecting off the water. It was all so peaceful and ordinary but tonight she had the feeling there was a coiled snake, about to strike in the middle of this happy family meal.

Julie shuddered.

Mr. Tracklin smiled down into her wide suspicious eyes.

She scowled back at him.

Something was simmering in those dark eyes as her hands clenched the platter bearing the salmon to the table.

Whatever it was, she showed no sign of being charmed by his noble presence. Was this animosity only for him or did she distrust all strangers?

As dishes were passed, the salmon served, bread buns

buttered, Andrew observed the unaffected zest for life Daniel Corwin's sister-in-law possessed. Her love for the Corwin family was obvious, but her reaction to him was puzzling. Perhaps she had no exposure to men in business suits with briefcases and cell phones, but he didn't think that was the problem. He bet she could hold her own in any company. She was no shrinking violet. It took incredible strength and resilience to live this kind of life. She had mentioned ruthless logging practices; perhaps it was his association with Tracklin's that riled her.

He glanced across the table at her helping Simon spread butter on his potatoes and grinned as she looked up to meet his eyes.

"My compliments to the chef."

"Thank you, Mr. Tracklin. It's hard to go wrong when everything is fresh from the garden."

The meal was splendid—delicate flavors, cooked exactly right, vegetables that had been in the ground only hours before. The season's first strawberries and the light sponge cake made an impressive dessert.

As Julie poured coffee, she whispered to Simon, who brought the candy box and carried it to each person in turn. Chocolates were a rare treat on Desolation Sound and each selection of 'the best one' took considerable time.

For someone with chocolate cravings, she was very generous with her limited supply. It didn't escape his notice— she took only one.

Later, after clearing the table and filling the pan with hot water, Julie began washing up, the three children dutifully standing beside her. She smiled at them. "This is a special day. You go and keep your Mom company."

Jake and Moira hesitated, but a deep voice settled the question. "Good idea. Run along, I'll help with the dishes."

Julie tensed as he stood close enough for her to feel his warm breath against the back of her neck. "That's not necessary," she squeaked. "Join the others. There's more coffee if you'd like."

He looked down his aristocratic nose at her. "And what about you? After preparing a grand meal, does Cinderella spend the evening in the scullery?"

He was making fun of her, daring her to argue. She remained silent, not rising to the bait, her hands in the soapy water, washing the dinner plates but itching to fling suds into his polite and charming face.

Picking up a dishtowel, he said, "Let me help." The words were spoken quietly, but with authority. He was telling her, not asking.

"Thanks," Julie accepted. She really couldn't do anything else without making a scene. "This is usually Anna's job, but as you can see, she's not able to do much, yet."

"Then let me pay for that splendid meal by helping the cook wash up."

They finished the dishes in silence as the Corwins sat around the wood stove, the soft light of oil lamps lighting their faces as Daniel read aloud a further chapter in the adventure story of sailing ships on the west coast.

Andrew wondered about 'Martin.' For an emotional woman, she didn't seem very excited about his letter; even *he* aroused more reaction than that. She wasn't subdued about her feelings for him.

He had many questions about Daniel Corwin's sister-in-law. She had an enchanting child-like quality that he suspected hid depths not associated with children.

He shook his head.

With a weekend of ledgers and management meetings ahead, Andrew bid the Corwins good-night. "Thank you for a delicious meal." He searched out the cook's dark-eyed face but her back was turned to him as she stoked the fire. Her well-worn jeans hugged the curves of her bottom as she bent over to pick another piece of wood from the wood

box. Only her backside and her wild curly hair received his
silent farewell and unspoken desire for a truce.

He refused Daniel's offer to walk with him to the helicopter. "It's started raining again. Stay round the fire with
your family. I'll fly you back to camp Monday morning;
I've left you stranded without your boat."

He waved to the group in the doorway as he walked to
the pasture where his helicopter sat. He wasn't satisfied
parting with Julie, so much left unsaid. But there was so
little chance—so much demanded her attention; the children, cooking, Anna. Plus, there was nowhere to get her
alone—one large room heated by the wood stove didn't
offer much privacy.

What was it about her that fascinated him, gave him the
urge to reach out and smooth back her riotous hair? Was
the remoteness of Desolation Sound having an effect on his
senses? "Stick to business," his father had told him. Well,
Daniel Corwin's sister-in-law was none of his business.

He sat rigidly in the pilot's seat as the helicopter gained
altitude to clear the trees on the hillside. His brooding eyes
became a somber gray as he admitted he was intrigued by
Julie—wholesome and free-spirited. She was not one to
flirt or encourage him.

And he must take the hint; stop thinking of her. Remember he was only here temporarily. There was no possibility
for a long-term relationship.

With the children tucked into bed, Anna relaxed into the
soft folds of the sofa, weary but content.

"How was your first helicopter flight?"

"Terrifying. The view was spectacular once I dared open
my eyes, but I couldn't feel comfortable up in the sky."

"It was fast."

"Thank heavens! I was in danger of throwing up."

Daniel squeezed his wife's hand. "You're a keen sailor,
never seasick, I can't believe flying turns your stomach."

"I felt so helpless. When I fall out of a boat I can float or swim but falling out of a helicopter leaves me no choice. I'd drop like a stone."

"Parachute lessons," Julie suggested.

"Don't even think it! You'd enjoy them, not me. I'm staying on the ground." She looked at her leg, unnaturally white after six weeks in a cast, so skinny the bones showed. "But first I have to build strength back in this leg."

Daniel sighed with relief, his wife was on the road to recovery, and they all depended so much on her calm, supporting presence. And they had Julie to thank for Anna's recovery—nursing her, keeping her spirits up and tackling the burden of everyday chores. A wordless message passed between them, gratitude was unspoken. They both loved Anna and needed each other's help but now the worst was over. Anna was mending.

Talk drifted to members of the planting crew, their families, new babies and activities over winter.

"Bruce Sorkin showed an unusual interest in us . . . puzzling. Mr. Tracklin's offer to fly us to Powell River surprised me too."

"Any changes since the father retired? A nurse at the hospital said her husband was threatened with a layoff. There were rumors of a strike closing down the woods."

"I heard that, too, but I didn't sense strike action. With the high cost of living, men are anxious to hang on to their jobs."

Daniel's voice lowered and his face looked troubled. "One bit of news upset me. Tracklin's plans to spray the woods with pesticides." His brows furrowed thinking of his homestead being sprayed with chemicals.

"Julie, what effect will aerial spraying have on us, the animals, the garden, Geraldine's milk?"

"Did you hear what they plan to use?"

"Some scientific name," Daniel recalled. "The one used against the spruce bud worm in eastern Canada."

Alarm glinted in Julie's eyes. "Without success," she snapped. "It's dangerous, Daniel. It's a health risk, shown to aggravate breathing problems, cause birth defects, pollute ground water . . . the list goes on. And it's all so unnecessary."

Daniel and Anna listened in silence.

"If the hillside behind our house is sprayed, our water would no longer be safe to drink?"

Julie nodded. It was criminal—the life they had toiled so long to create could be snuffed out at the whim of one powerful man. "Surely, Tracklin's can't be serious. They can't have researched it fully. Have they no concern for the environment?"

"It sounded like firm plans are in place," Daniel replied solemnly.

Worry etched deep grooves on all three faces as they sat motionless, with the gloom of defeat. It couldn't be happening in a place as remote as Desolation Sound. They had moved away from the city to raise their children in a place safe from things like this.

"What idiot sprays something so toxic when there's no evidence of insect damage? He's mad!" Julie was fired up to fight injustice and defend the helpless.

The Corwins were not hopeful. What chance did one small voice have against a giant lumber company? Profits came first, not the well-being of an insignificant family.

Julie's emotions contrasted with her philosophical brother-in-law but they both wanted the same thing—to keep Desolation Sound safe for the couple and their children and generations to come.

Julie was a glimmer of hope, her chemical expertise valuable to defend them against powerful odds. Perhaps an educated voice had a chance.

"Daniel, tell me all you know. Who's responsible?"

"Tracklin's son is behind the decision. He's ambitious,

ruthless and impressed by technology. His father was more sensible. Things changed for the worst when he took over."

"Unscrupulous," Julie rumbled beneath her breath. That Tracklin man needed to be set straight. She stroked her chin, concocting a plan that would cut the ground out from under him. A strong argument against spraying was forming in her mind. She could cite data and case studies and all the long-lasting effects of pesticides.

"Get me some paper. I hope there are saner minds on his board of directors. They must rethink their spraying program. I'll put together a protest that will open their eyes. If they have the ammunition, they can challenge his leadership. I'll give them plenty of ammunition."

Anna and Daniel exchanged knowing glances. Nothing stopped Julie when she was passionate about something. She wouldn't accept anything she felt was wrong. She would put up a tireless fight. They didn't underestimate her ability, going to bed encouraged that if anyone could, Julie would convince Tracklin's not to spray.

Absorbed in her tirade on paper, Julie didn't notice when they bid her good night. She was incensed; words flew from the tip of her pen. Experienced preparing scientific reports, she welcomed the challenge. She needed no reference texts to enumerate the facts she required. She had served on many committees to protect natural habitats, all the facts were fresh in her mind.

Moira crept down early Saturday morning for a drink of water and found Julie fast asleep on the sofa with a pen still clutched between her fingers. She blew out the oil lamp, pulled a blanket up over her aunt's shoulders, then tiptoed back to bed.

Julie woke much later to the smell of coffee.

"How's the mad scientist this morning?"

Rubbing sleepy eyes, Julie grinned. "Madder than ever. I got a great argument on paper—enough to persuade a lumber baron. I'll type it up to look official and then we can stop worrying. They can't choose dangerous chemical spraying when they've heard the rational case against it. They just can't!"

Daniel admired Julie's enthusiasm but he wouldn't rest easy until he heard it from the Tracklin directors that spraying was canceled. He wouldn't put it past them to dismiss a protest as irrational fear. Julie had a Ph.D. and impressive credentials, but would that be enough?

Guessing Daniel's thoughts, Julie added, "If the Tracklins won't listen, we have strong grounds for a court case against them." Her confidence gave Daniel fresh hope. Sometimes, a city girl was worth her weight in gold.

The typed report looked impressive and rang with authority, based in scientific fact. "What are the letters after J. Marantse?" Moira asked, reading over her parents' shoulders.

"I put those in to impress them with my qualifications. Those are my degrees."

"Degrees?" Moira repeated. "I don't see numbers to tell how many degrees."

Anna smiled at Moira's question. "Not temperature degrees on a thermometer, dear. Julie has university degrees; they show she studied chemistry for a long time."

"Oh . . . that makes more sense."

Julie looked at Daniel. "How do we get this into the right hands?"

"There's a mail link from the lumber camp to the head office. I can take it to camp Monday morning."

No more was said about the proposed threat to poison their life and dreams and destroy a cherished home. A lot was riding on the success of Julie's report. She had to get the support of Tracklin's on her side. She couldn't fail.

Sunday afternoon, Julie set off on a long walk along the shore, giving Daniel time alone with his family before resuming his tree planting the next morning.

Bright sun shone from a clear sky, a fresh salty breeze blew in from the sea and whitecaps topped the waves as Julie walked along the jagged shore, stepping over driftwood and stones, head down looking for treasures the sea had washed up.

It seemed far away from civilization, yet here it was being threatened with chemical pollution. With such sobering thoughts in mind, Julie climbed over barnacle-encrusted boulders and found a flat sun-baked spot on which to rest, brushed aside the broken clamshells and stretched out.

She laid back with her sweater for a pillow, inhaling the cool salt air, watching seagulls circling lazily in the distance, sun glinting white off the undersides of their wings. The rhythmic lapping of waves combined with the warm afternoon sunshine lulled her to sleep. Her anger had been vented as she wrote through the night, and now she drifted into peaceful sleep.

A white sail appeared to the south—a sailboat tacking back and forth into the wind, heading for the shelter of the cove. The sleek white boat, sail billowed out, sliced through the waves. A lone sailor sat aft at the tiller, one eye on the set of his sail and the other on the shore he was fast approaching. Something on the rocks caught his attention. He reached for his binoculars and took a closer look.

"Fancy that." The soft feminine form and dark curls were familiar to him—in fact, had haunted him all weekend.

He abandoned his office to go sailing, intent on banishing her from his mind in the exhilaration of sun, wind and fresh air. Now he was heading into a cove where she lay on the rocks. Fate wasn't letting him avoid her.

Andrew Tracklin lowered his mainsail, dropped anchor, threw his dingy overboard and rowed to the narrow strip of pebble beach.

Quietly, he climbed the rocky bluff, assured himself she wasn't hurt, only sleeping, then settled beside her.

He had long ago convinced himself that only an urban woman, accustomed to wealth and privilege, could fit into his life. Why was he attracted to this girl who was so much a part of this remote wilderness, so unlike the bored and bejeweled wives of his business associates? Here she slept, no makeup, no artificial eyelashes, just crazy wild curls and a genuine flush of health. Could her unaffected natural beauty survive in the hustle-bustle city? Or would she be eaten alive by the false glitter and fast pace?

He stretched out beside her, thinking of a pilot who married a peasant girl in Greece and found himself supporting her ailing parents, putting her brothers through school, and raising four children of his own.

The lure of flashing dark eyes was a temptation—one he'd be wise to avoid.

Julie stirred, her body lethargic in the warm sun. She stretched her cramped arms, feeling gritty sand against one hand but something soft and warm with the other. She shot up into a sitting position and whirled around.

"You!"

Andrew coolly looked back into her startled face, flushed pink from sun, and drowsy from sleep.

Julie took a deep breath, and raised her shoulders to ease the stiffness, indignant at the nerve of the man turning up here, while plotting to force the Corwins out by poisoning their surroundings. Did he have no heart?

She was very attractive, glaring at him, eyes flashing fire.

"Sorry to frighten you." His deep voice didn't sound the least bit apologetic. "I thought you might be hurt."

His expression was unreadable. Was he just being helpful? He sat there cool and unruffled in his pale blue shirt and white shorts, clean and pressed, unlike her, crumbled and windblown.

"Thank you," Julie said quietly, looking around for the helicopter that accompanied his presence but saw instead, a sailboat anchored in the cove. She intended to give him a piece of her mind but her delight at the lovely little boat outweighed her antagonism. It bobbed at anchor, on a tranquil blue sea, framed by the rocky bluffs and dense forest beyond. "A Thunderbird!" She didn't wait for his reply. "They're a joy, big enough for comfort, small enough for sailing single-handed."

Lowered lids concealed surprise in the shuttered blue eyes. Not only did she recognize the class of sailboat, she seemed knowledgeable and enthusiastic too.

"My feelings exactly."

"Anna and I sailed a lot in our youth, from a Sabot to a six-meter racing yacht. I've always loved Thunderbirds."

Remarkable as her sailing experience was, the phrase 'Anna and I' caught his attention. "You knew Anna as a child?"

Julie cast him a look of scorn. "Yes . . . since she was five years old . . . from the day I was born. She's my sister."

His features softened into a genuine smile, those blue eyes positively glowed, and frown lines dissolved into his tanned face. Julie stared at him in wonder. His megawatt smile was blinding.

"Didn't you know we're sisters?"

"I . . . I . . ." He stammered. "That is . . . Daniel referred to you as his sister-in-law. I thought that meant you were married to his brother." He added, "*My* sister-in-law is married to *my* brother. Moira mentioned you didn't have a husband but it never occurred to me you were Anna's sister." He raised outstretched hands. "I have a hard time sorting out relatives."

"Daniel doesn't have a brother."

He looked so pleased to hear this. Julie laughed.

He felt the need to explain. "It was a natural assumption; you were competent looking after children, cooking, running a household, and you must have had practice to do it so well." It was a new experience being on the defensive. This woman had a knack for unsettling him.

Julie enjoyed hearing him sputter. He didn't seem such a tyrant sitting here, in shorts, beside the sea, on sun-drenched rocks. He seemed almost human, an image not compatible with the Tracklin son Daniel talked about—the business machine without a heart.

"I may look competent to an untrained eye, but running a homestead is not something I have practice doing."

"You could have fooled me."

"Daniel's and Anna's lifestyle takes a lot of commitment. If we all lived as simply as they do, there would be far less strain on the earth's resources."

"I see your point. But not many of us could thrive in the demanding conditions the Corwins have."

"That's true. Daniel calls it 'walking softly on the earth—leaving no footprints.' We could all attempt to do that in our lives, if only in small ways."

"It's obvious you've given this a lot of thought."

"Our life depends on it, Mr. Tracklin."

The sun dropping closer to the horizon cast bands of gold across the water, signaling time to return and prepare dinner. Quickly standing and brushing sand off her clothes, Julie said, "I'd better be getting back." She picked up her sweater, shook it out and turned to retrace her path along the shore.

"Beautiful boat," she said absently as the setting sun bathed it in gold.

Unwilling to have her slip away when he still had so many questions, Andrew Tracklin blurted, "You're invited to come sailing, any afternoon."

Julie turned. "Anna couldn't take care of everything alone yet, not for another few weeks. Ask me again then. I might take you up on it."

He hadn't expected acceptance. "I'll do that." He gestured to the setting sun across the water. "I'll wait to sail into the sunset with you."

Julie shook out her mass of dark curls and tipped her

face up to meet those penetrating eyes. Although gifted with a silver tongue, Mr. Tracklin was rather subdued this afternoon, not the ambitious tycoon she'd imagined him to be. A man who enjoyed sailing couldn't be all bad. "Something to look forward to," she said dryly, more sarcastic than eager.

He reached out to help her clamber down over the rocks, his strong hand firmly grasping her much smaller one. Her defiant face did not deter him, he kept hold of her hand as they walked across the narrow stretch of beach to his dinghy.

Julie slipped her hand free and tucked it in her pocket. "Good-bye," she said. "If we don't get sailing before I go home, thanks for the offer." Giving him no chance to reply, she turned and walked quickly along the shore toward the Corwin house.

Before disappearing around the curving shoreline, she turned and waved. Andrew Tracklin stood beside his dinghy, swamped by a strange desire to run after her. He waved in reply, then slowly rowed out to his sailboat.

The way she kept him at arm's length was intriguing . . . there was some barrier between them . . . he didn't like being so forcefully dismissed. Was 'Martin' the reason she gave him the cold shoulder?

As Julie picked her way back along the shore, she pondered her encounter with Mr. Tracklin. Was that the same man intending to pollute the woods with chemicals, the same ruthless power who preferred machines to men? How could anyone who sailed that pretty little boat do such a thing?

She was confused. How could a man thoughtful enough to check on a person asleep on the shore, deprive hundreds of men their jobs? It made no sense. Daniel described the Tracklin son as selfish and unfeeling but this afternoon he behaved kind and considerate. Either the man had two sides or she was suffering from sunstroke.

His true nature would come to light tomorrow when her report was delivered to his office. If any compassion he displayed this afternoon was sincere, he'd respond immediately and the Corwins's home would be safe.

Julie tramped up the slope leading to the house, fingers crossed that her argument was strong enough to reach his heart—if he had one.

She said nothing about meeting Andrew in the chatter and bustle of preparing dinner. She wished she could reassure Daniel and Anna that all would be well, but so much depended on one powerful man caring enough to listen to reason, and humble enough to admit he was wrong.

Julie never did tell Anna about meeting Mr. Tracklin that afternoon; it seemed so unreal as if she'd dreamed it. She had never kept secrets from her sister. Would his offer to go sailing still be good after he read her report? Or would he dismiss her as a 'tree-hugger?'

Julie was up before dawn Monday morning, feeding the wood stove, heating water, then clomping across the yard wet with morning dew, to gather the chicken eggs. Back in Vancouver, she'd miss these simple chores but she'd love being back for the start of the symphony season. She missed the full orchestra sound of those evening concerts. Quiet was nice . . . but she missed music. She missed fresh orange juice too.

She slipped quietly into the house to find Daniel packing freshly washed clothes into his knapsack. "Morning, Julie."

She smiled from behind the bucket of water she'd brought from the well and he continued, "I can't thank you enough for being here, looking after Anna and the children. But you'll be wanting to get home soon, won't you?"

"I still have another month. Getting back into my city ways will take some doing after life here."

He laughed. "You mean you're willing to exchange your

sports car and nights on the town for milking goats and cooking on a wood stove?"

"I didn't say that."

"I know, Julie. I was teasing. You've been a good sport about all this, we'll miss you." He didn't say how surprised he was that a girl who'd lived in a large city all her life could adjust to life on Desolation Sound and never whine about how much easier life was in her high-rise apartment. "I'll be back a week from Wednesday. Let's put off talk about your leaving till then."

"Deliver that report this morning or it may be more than just me leaving." She remembered Mr. Tracklin was coming to helicopter Daniel back this morning. "You can give it directly to the ruthless Tracklin son this morning when he flies you back to camp."

Daniel looked puzzled. "You mean Andrew Tracklin, don't you?"

"Yes, Andrew Tracklin. Is there some other Tracklin son?"

"Yes. David. He's Andrew's older brother, the heartless business machine. He's the one behind all the plans for chemical spraying." He saw dismay on Julie's face. "I thought you knew. David Tracklin stays in the boardroom, he'd never lower himself to help an employee or dirty his hands in lumber camps."

"Oh," Julie groaned.

Daniel cocked his eyebrows, waiting for an explanation but Julie remained silent. "Oh . . . what?"

"Oh, I've been unfair to Andrew Tracklin, I've blamed him for his brother's nasty deeds. I've made a terrible mistake."

"Don't worry about it. He's a fair man; repaired most of the damage since he's been here. No one knows if David Tracklin intends to return, but I hope he doesn't."

"Where is he?"

"Rumor has it, he ran off with some nightclub singer and is living in Montreal."

Anna limped into the kitchen to join Daniel for breakfast. Julie discreetly picked up the milking pail and headed for Geraldine's pasture, leaving Anna some private time with her husband.

If possible, the ornery goat was glad to see her this morning, having kept their truce after that first disastrous milking. She no longer sidestepped, kicked, butted or tried to bite Julie, and for this Julie was grateful as she sat on the milking stool with her pail beginning to fill. A lump tightened in her throat as she heard the expected clatter but she couldn't stop milking halfway through.

When the helicopter dropped gently at the far end of the pasture, she was still at Geraldine's side. Andrew Tracklin had spotted her. He walked briskly, approaching the goat cautiously. His broad shoulders and tanned faced towered above the goat's scruffy body. His dark blond hair, bleached almost white in spots by the sun, was neatly combed, every hair in place. Inquisitive blue eyes peered over Geraldine to gaze into soft brown eyes shyly looking up at him.

A strange flush of warmth invaded the space between them.

"Good morning." The deep voice broke the early stillness, salted with the tang and chill of sea air.

Julie finished milking Geraldine with trembling fingers. "Good morning."

She was aware of his presence as she set the goat free to graze. A fluttering inside felt as though a thousand butterflies had taken flight within her.

He looked different this morning, no longer the ruthless man she'd wrongly assumed him to be. An apology was in order . . . she found it hard to find the words to make one. "I owe you an apology," she said softly.

Andrew raised an eyebrow, waiting for her to continue.

"Only this morning," Julie began, "I discovered you have an older brother . . . and he's the one responsible for Tracklin's policy. I've unjustly accused you of your brother's crimes." She looked up into his attentive blue eyes. "I'm sorry."

So that was why she had been so hostile. He beamed that megawatt smile and banished the early morning chill that had crept through Julie's bones.

"Apology accepted."

Julie awkwardly reached for the pail, sloshing milk over the rim onto her rubber boots.

Andrew removed the pail from her hands, never taking his eyes from hers. "There's a new movie showing in Powell River next week. Will you come to see it with me when I bring Daniel home?"

She was unprepared for this invitation. There she stood in grubby overalls, smelling like a goat, unable to string two words together, and catching sight of Daniel and Anna walking slowly toward the helicopter. With racing pulse, she lowered her head to avoid the scrutiny of those compelling eyes. He stood so close she could feel heat radiating from him but still Julie shivered.

Finally, she regained her voice. "I'd like that," she whispered. His warm smile trapped any apology or further explanations in her throat. She had a lot to say but no words came.

"I look forward to next Wednesday, then," he said.

Julie retrieved the milk pail from his hands, unaccountably dizzy. Missing breakfast might account for the swimminess in her head but she couldn't explain why her legs felt they were going to crumple beneath her.

They walked toward the helicopter, neither speaking but both filled with a thousand questions.

Daniel tossed his knapsack into the helicopter, embraced Anna and kissed her one more time.

Julie glanced at Andrew, frustrated they had so little time

and so little privacy. She'd blamed him for his brother's misdeeds. Now she wanted to set things straight but he was flying off. There was no time to talk. And she wanted to discuss the spraying with him too.

"I'll be in Vancouver later this week. Is there anything I can bring you?"

Touched by the thought, Julie was unaware of the wistfulness her smile conveyed. "There is one thing . . ." She hesitated. His calm attention encouraged her to go on. "We're out of cinnamon."

She peered up through her long lashes. "Just a little tin," she added. "Some recipes are boring without a little spice."

Andrew slipped into the pilot's seat beside Daniel, his eyes still on Julie's face. "I'll bring you that cinnamon." His deep voice sent shudders through her.

He raised his hand in a farewell gesture. It seemed a casual move but the look on his face and the way he stared right into her soul, made it an intimate contact.

Immediately, the helicopter roared into life and lifted up out of the pasture. Julie and Anna looked skyward as it became smaller and smaller, then disappeared from sight. Julie slowly raised her hand to brush hair out of her eyes. The day was warming up in the rays of the morning sun, but she felt strangely shaky as she gave Anna her arm for support and they headed back to the house, both lost in their thoughts.

Chapter Four

The next ten days dragged. It was like having thrown a grenade and breathlessly waiting for an explosion that never came.

By faithfully doing the exercises the doctor prescribed, Anna was gaining strength in her arm and leg and began taking over the cooking and cleaning. Julie did the outside chores and tended the garden, grateful for the daily exercise that kept her restless anxiety from taking over. She welcomed the constant activity and long hours spent over the steaming glass jars and canning kettle, preserving the vegetables being produced in abundance.

"Andrew invited me to the movies."

"Good. He seems a more sensitive man than his brother."

"I'm not sure. He's so confident and self-assured, his manners so smooth, I suspect they're not sincere, just well-practiced. I wonder if he's really that different from his brother."

Anna looked at her sister thoughtfully. "You deserve an evening out; I know this isn't your usual glamorous style of living—no dressing up, no evenings at the theater, no shopping trips or long chats on the telephone. An evening with Andrew Tracklin will give you a break and a chance to find out what he's really like."

"Then why the sad note in your voice?"

"Thinking . . . you'll soon be leaving us."

Julie put her arm around her sister as they stood together over the steaming canning kettle. "Haven't you had enough of your kid sister trailing after you?"

"We couldn't have made it without you these past months."

"Don't get maudlin on me. You did it all without me for years and you'll do just fine when I'm gone."

Anna sniffled. "I can't believe this. You're beginning to sound sensible. My little sister is growing up."

They laughed together. Anna never imagined Julie shouldering the responsibilities she had this past while, and doing such a good job of it. Life at Desolation Sound was going to have a giant piece missing when she left.

On Tuesday evening, Anna filled the water reservoir for washing hair. Toweling off her thick mass of wet curls, Julie froze, struck by an unsettling thought—she had no suitable clothes for going to the movies, no clothes suitable for going anywhere beyond the pasture. She'd worn through the knees of her pants, her shirts were faded, ripped and stained, and her shoes completely destroyed.

"I don't have anything to wear!"

"You have a closet full of designer clothes."

"But not here. I can't go to the movies tomorrow . . . not in overalls and rubber boots, smelling like a goat."

"Remember that pink sweater you sent for my birthday?"

Julie nodded.

"You could wear that and one of my long skirts."

Julie mulled the idea. "The theater will be dark, no one will notice what I'm wearing."

"I doubt that," Anna teased. "A certain Mr. Tracklin will notice."

"Oh, him . . . I doubt he notices such things."

* * *

By Wednesday, Julie alternated between being nervous and excited as she carried wood, gathered eggs, hauled water and urged the children through their lessons. She hadn't felt like this since that awful roller coaster ride Anna dared her to take. She hoped this time she could keep from turning green and throwing up.

It was late afternoon when the familiar helicopter noise broke into the soothing sounds of wind and sea as Julie and Anna prepared dinner. The three children dashed outside to greet their father. When they entered the kitchen, Andrew stood inside the doorway, his gaze settling on the soft pink sweater and the delightful feminine shape it covered. She seemed somehow out of place in this remote setting—a ridiculous thought because she was so obviously familiar with pioneer living.

Julie had been expecting him but not looking like he did. It was almost as though this evening was something special. He wore a dark suit, spotless white shirt and fine silk tie. He hadn't dressed casually. He made a movie in a small town seem as important as opening night at the opera. She was impressed . . . set off balance by the gesture. She could only stare, sweeping his long length from head to toe with appreciative eyes.

Anna broke the silence. "Will you join us for dinner? There's still time to make the movie."

"I'd be delighted." He smiled. Julie put her hand out to steady herself against the kitchen table.

He crossed the floor to stand beside her and pulled a small package from his jacket pocket. "I didn't forget. Every life needs a little spice."

The sultry voice hinted at a meaning more than the words expressed.

"Thank you," Julie stammered. Her eyes were caught in the glow of his and she couldn't look away. "I'll use it . . . sparingly. Too much can be . . . overpowering."

Andrew noticed she didn't blush, bat her eyelashes, or

pretend shyness. She was quick, her response refreshing—
like a tennis match—anything he threw her way, she threw
right back. This was no simpering girl in awe of the Tracklin name.

"I have something else." He produced a large package.

Julie was too surprised to object. She removed the wrapping from a familiar purple candy box, only this one was
enormous. Her eyebrows rose. "You must have bought out
the store!" She smiled, genuine pleasure filling her warm
brown eyes. "Thank you," she said, just barely above a
whisper. He'd given women diamonds and not gotten a
response like that. He felt warmth filling his chest as he
watched her.

Dinner was garden-fresh and delicious as usual, but
when dessert was finished and Julie rose to wash the dishes,
Anna pulled her aside.

"Not tonight, Julie. I'll do the dishes." Julie began to
protest but her sister cut her off. "The way Mr. Tracklin's
eyes are following you . . . he wants you alone. Don't keep
him waiting. Get your sweater, I'll clean up here."

Color flushed Julie's cheeks. She gave her sister a dis-
gruntled look but reached for her sweater.

Seeing Julie prepare to leave upset Simon. His usually
cheerful freckled face was sad, his big brown eyes near to
tears as he watched and worried. He was there when his
mother slipped on wet seaweed and fell. He saw her bleed-
ing and in pain lying on the rocks below. He'd watched
her closely ever since. Now he was afraid. He didn't want
Julie to go. What if she got hurt the way his mother did?

As if reading the child's thoughts, Andrew knelt down
and gently reassured him. "We're going to a movie, Simon.
I'll keep Julie safe."

It distressed Julie to see Simon so fearful; she thought
that was all past. The nightmares had ended . . . the tears
. . . and the clinging. She crouched down and kissed
Simon's cheek. The male scent of Mr. Tracklin's cologne

teased her nostrils as he was so close. His firm arm went around both her and Simon.

"She's our precious jewel," a tearful voice whispered.

"She's precious to me too," a much deeper voice replied.

Andrew straightened and took Simon's hand in his. "I'll take good care of her." Then he bowed and asked, "Do we have your permission?"

The little boy grinned and nodded, apprehension whisked away.

He trusted this man.

Julie swallowed the lump in her throat as she watched.

Walking toward the helicopter, Andrew noticed her thoughtful expression and asked, "Do all your gentlemen callers have to pass such inspection? I've been asked for my driver's license by doubting fathers but your nephew really put the pressure on."

The way he was studying her made her explain, "Simon feels a bit protective; he was upset to see his mother hurt, now he worries when anyone is out of sight for long."

They reached the helicopter and he helped her into the passenger seat. "You handled Simon nicely . . . thank you for understanding."

He smiled as he reached across to buckle the seat belt around her. His arm brushed lightly against her. Julie trembled and her stomach fluttered.

"Cold?"

"No, frightened."

"Don't be." He squeezed her hand gently. "I plan to keep that promise to Simon."

That was reassuring. In minutes, the helicopter lifted off the ground smoothly like a feather on the breeze.

"You can open your eyes now."

Warily, Julie blinked. She saw the neatly laid out homestead below, green forest rising up the hillside behind and the murky blue sea spreading out in front. "Beautiful," she exhaled on a long-held breath.

The pilot couldn't agree more. He associated her with wind in her hair, freedom, and wilderness. Sadly, he knew a wild forest flower couldn't be transplanted to city streets and still thrive.

"You obviously love this untamed landscape."

"I do . . . and I'd fight to my death to keep it unspoiled."

He was about to ask where her home was when she left Desolation Sound, but the outline of buildings in the distance signaled their arrival.

The excitement of dropping out of the sky quite pleased Julie. She could get used to such hassle-free travel. No stop lights, traffic jams, blaring horns.

"The movie theatre is a short walk in that direction," Andrew gestured. "We have plenty of time."

The man was so composed, Julie couldn't read his thoughts or even imagine what he was thinking. Walking quietly beside him, she stifled aimless chatter because of his commanding presence. She feared she would give herself away in nervous babbling. He saw her as a simple backwoods woman and she didn't know where to begin telling him she wasn't what she seemed—she had another life and a successful career in Vancouver. Asking about the proposed spraying was out of the question. He would wonder how she knew about it. He was a perceptive man and she didn't want to spoil this rare evening out in arguments and heated debate when he discovered her part in opposing the reckless use of chemicals. Lumber barons weren't known for their environmental concerns.

As if reading her mind, he asked, "Have there been any strangers around Desolation Sound lately?"

"No. Why?"

"We received an impressive plea to stop aerial spraying, so knowledgeable, the author must be very familiar with this area. Did you see anyone inspecting the woods?"

Julie lowered her head, unwilling to reveal her emotions.

"Only you," she replied as calmly as her tightly reined hope would allow.

"I'd like to meet the man who wrote that report; clever, with common sense and a fine turn of phrase. He made the entire board question whether chemical spraying is necessary. My older brother, David, had done little research on how dangerous the spraying could be. The board of directors has had its eyes opened to the long-term effects. We have a responsibility to protect the earth . . . not just harvest timber."

"I wholeheartedly agree," Julie said with feeling.

Delighted, she itched to throw her arms around him, but she restrained herself and drew in a deep breath. The sea breeze smelled strongly of fish and salt water, but she didn't care—Desolation Sound had a good chance of remaining untouched!

With eyebrows scrunched down over piercing blue eyes, he studied her closely. He noticed the happiness turning up the corners of her mouth and lighting her large brown eyes. She must have strong feelings about the use of chemicals; an evening at the movies couldn't be responsible for that glow of excitement on her face. His questioning gaze was hard to avoid.

Julie burbled into speech. "I'm glad there'll be no spraying." She said it innocently, trying hard not to gloat over her success.

"Hold on. I didn't say there would never be any spraying. The board is reconsidering—the delay may merely be temporary. We're tracking down the chemist who wrote that report. A good man like that would be welcome at Tracklin's; we need professional expertise."

Julie nodded. Now was the time to identify herself as the author of the report . . . but the words didn't come. Her mind was occupied, planning a way to get to Vancouver, to speak to Tracklin's board of directors and convince them they must cancel chemical spraying permanently.

She smiled, thinking of the evidence she would present. No rational person could consider poisoning the environment when they heard all the arguments against it.

Andrew made no comment, merely noted the look on her face, much like his mother's when she was plotting some nefarious scheme. They continued walking the short distance to the theatre. He would find out in time, but for now, he wouldn't ask.

The silence gave Julie a chance to consider what he had said. Of course she was ecstatic the spraying was being questioned, but that bit about a *man* writing the report was insulting. It made her angry to think Mr. Tracklin assumed only a man had brains enough to be educated or make a convincing argument.

She entered the small movie theatre at his side, wondering how he'd react to discover a woman had written that report. Would it make any difference to him?

She could only wonder. It was on the tip of her tongue to tell . . . but the movie was about to begin. There was no opportunity to expose the truth.

The plush red seats were well worn but very comfortable as they settled in. Once the lights dimmed, Julie was immediately absorbed by the suspense even before the opening credits vanished from the screen. It had been ages since she'd seen a movie.

Her rapt attention didn't go unnoticed in the semi-darkness, shuddering as each clue to the mystery was set in place. As tension built and violence slashed across the screen, Julie gasped wide-eyed, and hid her head against the shoulder beside her, shielding her eyes with her hand.

Andrew protectively drew her close against him, more entranced by the action beside him than that on the screen.

Julie relaxed, nestled against his broad chest, her face burrowed in the safety of his jacket. "Tell me when it's over."

She could feel his laughter in the wobbly rise and fall of

his chest but she refused to look until the scary part was over. Andrew's hand stroking her back through the fluffy wool of her sweater felt so comforting, she didn't care if she missed the rest of the movie.

He was the one who never did see how the movie ended. He was so distracted by the silky head of curls snuggled under his chin and the intriguing woman first hostile then trusting, a grand mix of emotions. He liked the feel of her against his chest, as she watched the movie end.

When the house lights went on, Andrew was loathe to remove his arm but Julie stirred and rubbed her eyes; she stiffened and pulled away.

Her eyes adjusted to the light and she prickled at the look on that handsome face. It was as though he'd uncovered a secret she had carefully concealed.

Little did he know all the revelations left unspoken. She was embarrassed, her vulnerable side exposed. His unruffled composure was in sharp contrast to her emotional lack of control. No wonder he thought only *men* could write intelligent reports.

She looked down at her feet but followed as he took her hand and led her from the brightly lit theatre into the darkening summer night. She expected to hear some caustic comment. But none came. The man at her side walked with long slow strides, up the slope toward the helicopter pad, his thoughts to himself, his face a mask of cool reserve.

After Ian's critical remarks, Andrew's silence was hard to decipher. She imagined all sorts of nasty things he must be thinking, then remembered Anna's lecture. *That's in the past. Not all men are like Ian!*

Of course she was embarrassed, flinging herself over a virtual stranger in a dimly lit theatre. But it wasn't possible to be controlled and sensible while watching a terrifying murder on screen.

Julie bit her lip, feeling strangely tearful. Why didn't he say what was on his mind?

An infuriating smile warmed her as she defiantly lifted her head.

He thought she had little experience with evenings out and fast-paced movies aimed at city folk hardened against crime and violence. He found such naive innocence touching. The accusation in her eyes had him puzzled.

"What have I done to have you looking at me like that?"

Her mouth opened but she said nothing. Two long firm fingers tipped her apprehensive face up to his. "Never apologize for being sensitive. You reminded me how callous life in the city can become. There are so many distractions, we forget the simple things . . . the important things."

He kissed her gently, the bright light above shining down on her lustrous curly hair. Reluctantly pulling away, he whispered, "Don't ever change."

Julie came back to reality with a thump. What did he know about her? Certainly not the truth. He was building an image of her that wasn't real and she didn't have the heart to destroy his dream. Change? Ha! She wasn't what he thought. But when he looked at her the way he was now, she didn't have the courage to tell him it was all an illusion.

Carefully, he helped her into the helicopter and buckled her seat belt, the brush of his hand across her leaving tingles, like the prickles a stinging nettle left when she grabbed it by mistake. After slipping in behind the controls, he leaned closer to say, "I must get Simon's precious jewel home quickly. I promised."

Some jewel, she thought to herself—tarnished beyond belief, afraid to tell him the truth about herself, yet guilty for leading him on. How pathetic!

When the helicopter set down in Geraldine's pasture, Julie was off balance, ashamed of herself for lacking the courage to tell Andrew who she really was. She needed time to talk; there were so many misunderstandings between them.

And the hole she had dug herself into just kept getting deeper.

But he gave her no chance to discuss the things troubling her. He guided her firmly toward the house, then said softly, "Good-night, Julie."

His finger lazily traced the outline of her ear, making Julie quiver at his feather-light touch. He gently kissed her lips, holding her in the circle of his arms as her hands inched up across his chest.

"Good-night," she whispered. "Thanks for taking me to the movie. Although I love it here on Desolation Sound, it was a treat to get away, however briefly."

She wanted to say much more. She had no idea how sad the look in her soft brown eyes was.

Julie slipped inside the house, thankful for the lantern Anna had left burning low.

A few minutes later, pouring water into the basin to wash, she heard the clatter of a helicopter fade into the still night air.

Impossible, she thought. *He thinks I'm something I'm not. Whenever I start to explain I end up further from the truth.*

Oh, well, I don't suppose it matters. Once I slip away home, our paths will never cross again.

By his usual standards, it was still early when Andrew returned to the house the Tracklin Company maintained in Powell River. The couple that acted as caretakers had left fresh coffee, sandwiches and a selection of cakes on a covered tray in the spacious kitchen.

He poured coffee and carried it through to his study. Sitting behind the solid desk, he clicked on his computer and studied the day's e-mail messages. It was unnecessary for him to stay on in Powell River; he was expected back in Vancouver yesterday but he put off his return, claiming difficulties in the woods—difficulties long settled. The

Tracklin Company was thriving, business was progressing smoothly and no representative from the head office was needed here, but still Andrew Tracklin remained in Powell River.

His parents were hosting a celebration dinner this weekend for his brother and Monique to honor their wedding; his presence was required. He daydreamed about taking Julie to such a gathering; he wanted her to meet his family. What would she make of his parents' lifestyle? Would she be in awe of their wealth and possessions? He didn't think so—she was so natural and not judgmental. Her values were not those affected by things money could buy.

Perhaps this wasn't the time to introduce her to his life in Vancouver. After all, it was David's big moment, all the fuss and congratulations. He'd wait for a simpler time, gradually expose her to his parents, society life, the noise and pollution of a large city. He'd do it slowly, not scare her off at one huge formal banquet.

Next, he listened to his telephone messages—business conferences, dinner invitations, the airline wanting confirmation of his resignation. He'd like to telephone Julie this evening and have a long chat, ask all those things he never had a chance to. What were her likes and dislikes? Did she go to movies often? Where did she live when she wasn't at the Corwins'? Did she work? Was she involved? Who was 'Martin?' But no telephone lines stretched to the homestead on Desolation Sound. He put his coffee mug down and picked up the telephone.

"Yes, Mother. I got your message. I've been delayed . . . I want to get in a bit of sailing."

"By yourself, dear? That will be nice."

"No . . . actually, I've invited someone."

"A young lady? Does she enjoy sailing?"

"Yes, Mother . . . quite an accomplished sailor, I believe."

"That should be a treat for you." Mrs. Tracklin was brimming with curiosity, but no hint of it was revealed in her quiet voice. "You'll be back in time for the banquet, won't you?"

"I'll be there, and toast the newly married couple."

"I knew we could count on you, Andrew. Your support means so much to David."

"I'll see you in a few days' time."

He made more calls, leaving instructions for his secretary, arranging his following week, and confirming business appointments.

That done, he walked through the silent house to pour himself more coffee. He'd half planned to bring Julie here after the movie but he'd lost his nerve as they walked back to the helicopter. He didn't want to rush things.

This opulent house furnished in grand style might set her off. He wanted to get to know her without flaunting his moneyed background. He wanted her to trust him. Would she be intimidated by this modern kitchen, the well-stocked freezer or his Jaguar in the garage?

He wanted to know more about Julie. If the weather held, he'd take her sailing. Corwin was home to look after his wife and family. One thing he did know—the woman appreciated a beautiful sailboat when she saw one.

He switched on the television to watch the late news, wondering what Julie was doing. Without electricity, she couldn't watch TV or listen to music or talk on the telephone. He was curious. She led an unusual life on Desolation Sound but she didn't seem deprived in any way. In fact, he'd swear her life was more fulfilling without all those distractions.

Most women he knew gloried in the limelight, they needed lots of people around them, loved to be the center of attention. Somehow he knew Julie wouldn't be like that. He could see her having a quiet chat over tea with his mother, without any of the meaningless flattery, and phony kisses he found so distasteful.

He rinsed his coffee mug and set it in the dishwasher.

A day's sailing, he decided—exactly what was needed.

Chapter Five

The raspberries ripened all of a sudden, red and plump, and they demanded picking immediately. Julie, Jake and Moira stood amidst the tall canes, filling buckets with ripe raspberries. This year's crop was enormous.

The morning sun gave promise of a scorching afternoon in spite of the cooling breeze from the water. For this reason, Julie had started early, her cotton shirt already sticky against her body, damp with perspiration. Jake and Moira had slowed their rate of picking, and were now sitting at the end of the row with red-stained fingers and mouths, eating the largest, most tempting berries.

"If you carry those to the house, I'll finish up here."

"Do you think there's enough for a pie?"

"More than enough, Jake, enough for many pies and jam and more to pick again tomorrow if this sunny weather lasts."

The children carried full raspberry pails back to the house as Julie bent low, seeking out the fat berries hanging in clusters hidden under the leaves. Her fingers, also, were stained red and her knees were clumped with dirt from kneeling on the ground. Her cutoff jeans were hardly decent, so thin in spots they were almost transparent. Thankfully, Geraldine and the chickens scratching around the garden cared nothing for how a person was dressed. High fashion wasn't practical in a farmyard. Still, she longed for some clothes that weren't threatening to fall apart on the next washing. She felt guilty having such selfish thoughts— the most important thing was getting Anna back in full health, not making a fashion statement in the raspberry patch. She wiped her sticky fingers on her jeans and finished picking the rest of the berries.

Before noon, Julie had rolled out piecrusts and two raspberry pies were baking in the oven. The kitchen was sweltering from the heat of the wood stove, even with all the doors and windows thrown open to catch the wind blowing in off the sea. Perspiration glistened on her face and made her damp shirt cling like wet Kleenex. Hot and sweaty, she smoothed her dripping hair back off her face.

"How was the movie last night?"

"Gory in spots—but well written."

"Is that all you're going to tell me?" Anna watched her sister mashing juicy raspberries and measuring them into a large pot for making jam. "What about Andrew Tracklin? Is he all business like his brother?"

"I'm undecided." Julie poured boiling water over the jam jars to sterilize them. Clouds of steam rose to heat her already flushed face. It was like a sauna in the kitchen.

Anna had never seen Julie so close-mouthed. "What's to decide?"

"He's very reserved and in control. I'm never sure what he's thinking."

"He's not like Ian, if that's what you're afraid of."

Julie stirred the berries vigorously. "I don't know." She hesitated and kept her eyes on the pot, not looking up to see Anna's frustration at her brief answers.

"What about chemical spraying? Daniel heard nothing more, did Andrew mention it?"

"It's canceled for the time being." Julie carefully measured sugar to add to the almost-boiling raspberries.

"Really?" Anna squealed. "That's wonderful!" She clapped her hands together, splattering water droplets onto the stovetop where they sizzled and quickly turned to steam.

"The board of directors needs more convincing but I'm sure I can get a hearing with them when I return to Vancouver, and cement my case."

"Did Andrew discuss your report with you? What did he think about your reasons for opposing?" Anna was closely watching the paraffin melting atop the stove, not letting it get so hot it burst into flame. She didn't see Julie shrug and look sheepish.

"We didn't talk about it."

"What!" Anna moved the melted wax to the coolest edge of the stovetop. "You didn't talk about it! Our whole future depends on the spraying being stopped." She stared at Julie in amazement. "How did he react when he found out you're a chemical engineer?"

Julie poured the measured sugar into the rapidly boiling raspberries, stirring constantly with a long wooden spoon to keep the bottom from scorching. "I didn't tell him."

"You didn't tell him?" Anna readied the jam jars for filling, setting them out neatly on a folded towel. "Then what did you talk about?"

"There wasn't much time for talking, what with the movie and all." Julie ladled the cooked jam into jars while Anna wiped the rims and poured on the melted paraffin. "I think he assumes I'm this simple creature who's never seen a flush toilet or a light bulb."

The ruby-red jars of jam were set aside to cool and Anna stared at her sister. "He can't think that!"

"Well, look at me, Anna—like something the cat's dragged in. And he's seen me milking a goat, baking bread, digging potatoes—hardly sophisticated city things. What else could you expect him to think?"

"You didn't set him straight?"

"I didn't have the chance."

"That doesn't sound like you."

Julie poured soapy water into the jam pot and began washing up. "Well, this whole setting, living here without central heating or electricity, cooking, gardening, tending animals—none of it sounds like me. He just got the wrong impression. I'm not trying to deceive him, there's just no evidence of how I normally live." Julie scrubbed the pot until it shone. "And the more it goes on, the harder it is to tell him otherwise."

"He must suspect you're not some uneducated pioneer from the north woods."

"What does it matter? I'll never see the man again once I return home. Let him think what he likes—it makes him happy. It's all just a fleeting encounter . . . instantly forgotten . . . the second we leave Desolation Sound."

Anna eyed her sister suspiciously. It was unlike her to be anything but honest and open.

"I don't feel good about this. It's going to backfire on you."

"What's the worst that can happen? He'll discover I'm not what he thought. Big deal! I'm a novelty, something unusual . . . like writing in the sand, washed away when the tide comes in."

Anna saw the sadness in her sister's eyes and heard the wobble in her voice. She said nothing more. *That Ian Sutherland has a lot to answer for if he's the one who put all this self-doubt in Julie's mind. It isn't like her to be so unsure of herself.*

The raspberry pies sat cooling on the table, and makings for potato salad had boiled and were cooling beside them. No more wood was fed into the stove and the kitchen could blissfully cool down for the rest of the day.

"That's it for today's cooking." Julie let out a long breath, blowing the wisps of damp hair off her forehead and wiping her hands down the sides of her berry-stained shorts. "Race you to the water for a swim in the sea."

"Sounds heavenly. I'm so hot and sweaty; I don't care how cold the water is, but skip the race part. I need help to get there without crutches."

Clothes and all, the two sisters swam in the chilly salt water, washing away the morning spent sweating over a hot stove and rinsing away all traces of raspberry stains and garden dirt.

Daniel and the children appeared from behind the shed where they'd been stacking firewood to dry for winter. Daniel came down to the water's edge and helped Anna ashore and slowly back to the house, soaked to the skin and dripping a trail of salt water drops that quickly evaporated in the sun directly overhead.

Julie remained in the water, swimming out farther, then floating on her back, luxuriating in the refreshingly cool water, looking up into a brilliant blue sky with only the tiniest wispy clouds scudding across it.

She'd told Anna the truth. Would Andrew want to know the real Julie Marantse? It was all so complicated. A lot of men were uncomfortable with successful women . . . she had nothing to apologize for . . . but she'd learned to play down her achievements . . . crazy . . . she was fierce and confident . . . yet here she was holding back.

Perhaps she was just playing it safe . . . not wanting to upset the balance here on Desolation Sound . . . afraid to endanger her sister's family and the life they had chosen. She pushed the troubling thoughts away and let the chilly water wash over her.

She didn't see the billowing white sail approaching from the south. By the time Jake called, "Julie, lunch is ready," it had noiselessly pulled in alongside the Corwins' dock and its lone occupant was securing a mooring line.

Julie swam to shore, a strong swimmer from years of practice, then stood and walked in the last few yards. Her wet shirt and shorts, worn paper-thin, were plastered to her shapely figure. She reached up to drag the hair off her face and wring the seawater out of it. She didn't realize how this movement emphasized her chest and narrow waist but it didn't go unappreciated by the sailor on the dock.

Shaking water droplets off like a dog, Julie wished she'd brought a towel. Her ears were popping, filled with water, and mud was going to stick to her walking across the dry dirt with wet feet.

Startled, she inhaled quickly and nearly fell flat back into the water when a familiar deep voice said, "Allow me."

There stood Andrew Tracklin, sun-bleached hair neatly combed, crisp white sailing clothes dry and freshly laundered, holding out a big fluffy towel.

Gratefully, Julie accepted it, rubbing herself dry, then wrapping it self-consciously around herself. She rubbed her cheek against its softness, recognizing the scent of fabric softener, clothes dryer—a reminder of city life.

"Thank you."

"Not everyday I see Venus rising from the sea."

Julie smiled at the reference. "But would an artist have offered her a towel?"

"An artist, no; but a gentleman, most definitely."

"Jake called me for lunch. Will you join us?"

He kept pace beside her as she walked gingerly over pebbles and rough ground in her bare feet. "My name is Andrew. Unless you call me that, I will have to call you Miss . . . ?"

Not willing to reveal her surname and be identified as the author of the report before having a chance to explain, Julie quickly diverted him. "We baked fresh raspberry pies this morning. You're in for a treat."

He noted she avoided giving him her full name but

thought nothing more of it. One so natural and unspoiled surely had nothing to hide.

After a lunch of sandwiches, raspberry pie and lemonade, Andrew addressed the Corwins. "Can you spare Julie this afternoon? I offered to take her sailing."

Before he could say another word, Anna responded, "Great idea! Daniel's here to help if I'm stuck and Julie would love a sail."

Julie glowered at her sister, wondering if anyone was going to ask her opinion. After all, she was the one being sent off to sea with Andrew Tracklin. Didn't she get any say in the matter?

Apparently not.

"Good. It's great sailing weather, the wind is up and the sky is clear. We'll head north toward the marine park. We should be back by nightfall."

He looked at Julie in disreputable shorts and scruffy shirt, not seeming to care how she was dressed. "Ready?"

With no excuses, no previous engagements, no decent clothes to change into, no way to avoid the invitation, and the Corwins seemingly anxious to have her gone, Julie resigned herself, shrugged, then nodded. A day's sailing was hard to resist.

The little craft handled flawlessly, responsive to the tiller, light and buoyant as it cut through the sea. Her hair tied back with a bit of nautical braid, the wind fanning her face and her legs curled up under her well-worn faded shorts, Julie held the tiller on course and gloried as the filled sails pulled the sleek boat nearer the area set aside as a marine park.

Andrew Tracklin occupied himself with the winch, tightening the sail, then going below storing provisions and checking the chart. But all the while, his attention was focused on the fresh, unaffected woman who reveled in the joy of sailing. Her glow of health and vitality was his undoing. He didn't trust himself to sit beside her. She was too good to be true—a woman who genuinely loved sailing and was an expert at it, besides.

Julie tacked and came about, sailing offshore away from the rocks and shallow water. She did it so smoothly; Andrew was impressed. She was no novice, a delight to watch.

They dropped the sail and bobbed at anchor some distance from the few other boats in the bay. Julie was reluctant to go ashore, she'd come barefoot and wasn't prepared for hiking. Besides, she loved being out on the water; it brought back so many happy memories.

With two mugs of tea and a box of biscuits, Andrew sat opposite her.

"Milk and sugar?"

"Milk, please." Julie took the mug and warmed her fingers round it. Her happy face shone. "A mug of hot tea, a stiff breeze and a glorious little sailboat—heaven!"

"Indeed."

Julie helped herself to the sweet biscuits and leaned her head back to soak up the sun as she savored them.

"Have you lived all your life near the sea?"

"Mostly. Grandfather designed and built boats, so sailing was part of life for as long as I can remember."

"Not a usual pursuit for girls."

"Grandfather may have wanted grandsons, but Anna and I are what he got. He had us swimming and sailing as soon as we could walk."

"And your parents?"

"They divorced when I was three. I never saw my father after that and my mother wasn't comfortable around boats. She sailed with us occasionally but she was never enthusiastic. She would rather be tending her flower garden."

"Your grandfather trained you well. You're the most competent crew ever to board this ship."

This was the first she had talked about herself and he wanted to continue the conversation. She wasn't a woman to prattle on, boring him with all the petty details of parties, clothes, and acquaintances. She said so little . . . it whetted his appetite. He wanted to know more about this elusive woman. But she looked at the clouds forming to the south and said, "We'd better head back. We have to tack into the wind and it might take a while."

Reluctantly, he stowed the empty mugs in the galley. He brought a bulky sweater back on deck with him, a rich red shade like vintage port. "You might need this. From the chill in the air and the look of those clouds there's rain coming."

Julie pulled it on over her head, rolled up the sleeves so her hands were visible, then let it settle around her thighs where it reached almost to her knees. It had the scent of male cologne and she inhaled it so unselfconsciously, Andrew shuddered at the unintended intimacy of her action. Her innocence aroused him.

Gray clouds filled the blue sky and the wind gusted and became stronger as they sailed back. The sea, at first smooth, then choppy, was now rough with high waves. It had changed from sparkling blue to muddy gray, mirroring the darkening sky above. Salt spray splashed over the bow as the little boat cut through the whitecaps. Rather than turning green with seasickness, Julie was nimbly moving across the deck, checking the rigging and adjusting the sail. She wasn't complaining about the cold, the wet, the ship's movement, or the lack of a large party of sailing companions.

"I gather you're no stranger to storms."

"Oh, I've seen plenty. Once off Dixon Entrance we suddenly hit such gale force winds I was thrown overboard."

"Wearing a life jacket?"

"No, rain slicker and rubber boots. They started to fill with water, get heavy and drag me down, so I kicked them off. My rain pants were filling with water, too, so I undid the clasps and let them drift away. Grandfather was way

off in the distance turning the boat around and I was starting to get cold."

"What happened?"

"Two elderly fishermen saw me go overboard and ma-
neuvered alongside me. They threw a life ring and began
to pull me up. When they saw my bottom half was naked,
they dropped me right back into the cold sea."

"Did your grandfather get back to save you?"

"No, the fishermen overcame their modesty long enough
to haul me aboard." Julie grinned. "Perhaps the threats and
salty language that passed between my chattering blue lips
changed their minds."

A full laugh, the kind that reverberated from his chest
and reached all the way up to his eyebrows, filled the small
space aft, near the tiller.

"Are you up to taking over the helm now?"

"I'd love to."

"Not so fast. First put on this life jacket." He handed her
the bulky orange vest and saw that it was properly fastened.
"I'm going below to heat us some supper. We're making
good time, we'll be back before nightfall."

He brought steaming bowls of beef stew and slices of
buttered bread on deck and took over the tiller.

Julie was hungry and immediately tasted the hot stew.
"Delicious." She chewed and swallowed. One would think
she was dining at a four-star restaurant. She noticed him
watching her and felt she must explain. "It's a delight to
have something I didn't cook myself. I'm getting tired of
my own cooking. Anna gives good advice and helps as
much as she can, but it's not the same as someone else
actually preparing a meal."

Andrew watched her eating and enjoying the food, unaware of the first cold drops of rain splattering her wild
tangle of hair. Simple, natural pleasures—the woman was
a treasure. He'd spent fortunes on gourmet meals that diet-

ing women picked at and left uneaten. His crew had a healthy appetite.

"The rain is starting. If you go below and tidy up, I'll have us in to Corwin's dock before the worst of it hits."

Julie washed up their dishes in the efficient galley, then padded about in her bare feet, inspecting the fine woodwork with the eye of a shipbuilder's granddaughter.

"Land ho," came the call from on deck. Andrew was lowering the sail. Automatically, Julie picked up the mooring line and stationed herself at the bow, ready to jump onto the dock when near enough.

With the boat snugly moored, she removed the life jacket and handed it to Andrew to stow in its locker. The rain was falling steadily now. They ran up the slope to the house, his arm around her waist, uncaring of the pelting rain.

"Great. You're back! It sounds like a wet one out there." The Corwins were sitting playing Scrabble and eating cookies.

"Have you had dinner?"

"Yes, Anna. The Thunderbird has a great galley, you'd love it, well stocked." The two sisters began to chatter about the boat and sailing, oblivious to anyone else in the room.

Daniel moved the plate of cookies closer to Andrew and motioned for him to take a chair. "Those two will talk sailing for hours. Try a cookie . . . oatmeal raisin . . . Julie's favorite."

"I'd think sailing's a valuable skill in a setting like this."

"More than a skill with those two . . . it's an obsession."

"Julie handled my boat like an expert. I was very impressed."

Daniel laughed. "I bet she didn't mention she and Anna won the Swiftsure . . . twice."

Andrew, eating his way through the plate of cookies, shook his head.

"They've got trophies," Jake piped up. "Want to see them?"

Andrew admired the winning cups and plaques the children pulled out of a cupboard. "Remarkable!" The woman was full of surprises. What other accomplishments had she neglected to mention? He watched her across the room intently sharing the day's sailing with her sister.

Julie and Anna, still discussing the merits of Andrew's boat, noticed the children dragging out the trophies and groaned.

"Put those away. They're ancient history."

"But, Mom, you're still the best sailor. Isn't that right, Dad?"

Daniel grinned. "The best!"

He looked at Anna with such a loving expression it was almost embarrassing to be in the same room.

Andrew was well aware of the lack of privacy in the Corwins' home. He'd like to get Julie alone to say good-bye, to tell her he was returning to Vancouver to take over his brother's place in the family business. He had no more reason to stay on Desolation Sound.

He wanted to invite her to visit his home in Vancouver . . . but she was needed here, far from the city, secure in the love of her family. It would take time for her to adjust to his lifestyle . . . if ever she could. Did he have the right to uproot her from all that was familiar? She was so passionate about protecting this wilderness area.

Getting Julie alone was impossible; he settled for shaking Daniel's hand and hugging Anna and the children.

"I'm going back to Vancouver in the morning. My business here is complete. It's been a pleasure meeting you."

His eyes lingered on Julie. He'd made his decision. He couldn't take a wildflower and expect it to grow in concrete. She would remain in his memory, windswept, lovely, and free. He had no right to deprive her of the natural surroundings in which she thrived. No right at all.

Subdued, she thanked him politely for taking her sailing, while the Corwins stood beside her and the three children bobbed for position by the door—no chance for any personal final words, no explanations, no hugs, not even a kiss on the cheek.

Andrew stepped into the rainy evening, turned and waved one last time at the six people in the doorway, then sprinted to the dock.

On the lonely trip back in the empty sailboat, he missed the lilting voice and laughter of the best crew ever to board his ship. He would remember her graceful movements and ease in setting the sails, her joyous cheer when the wind gusted strong and the boat leaned precariously to starboard. That beautiful woman would haunt this ship. And more.

With only the sounds of wind and sea for company, he agreed with Captain Cook.

Desolation Sound tears out a man's heart and leaves him desolate.

It was well named.

Chapter Six

Rebecca Tracklin surveyed the ballroom—linen table-cloths, family silver, fine china, delicate crystal, and elegant flowers arranged in pewter bowls. The guests were seated and dinner was ready to be served. She gave a signal to the headwaiter and the serving staff filed in quickly and silently with the first course.

The exquisite meal and flawless presentation were wasted on her new daughter-in-law, a voluptuous woman with a too-loud voice, in a too-tight dress, and a much-too-vulgar way of speaking.

Ever a woman of kindness and concern for her guests, the elderly woman kept her opinions to herself, welcoming David's new wife into her family and circle of friends with a gracious warmth.

By neither word nor gesture did she reveal her secret wish for a daughter-in-law she could share her interests with—an interest in gardening, a love of classical music, and an appreciation of fine art. She had yet to find any area of interest she and Monique shared, unless it was their love for David. And even that was in doubt. The way Monique gushed about the expensive gifts David had given her, the money he spent and the price tags on everything she fancied, Mrs. Tracklin questioned whether the woman's love was for her son or for the things his money could provide. She hoped she was wrong . . . for David's sake.

Good manners prevented any of these thoughts from surfacing as she wished the young couple happiness and said nothing about the low-cut dress that put more of Monique on view than Rebecca Tracklin felt proper.

David had made his choice, and as a good mother she would do nothing to cause him pain. She welcomed his wife with all the graciousness she could muster. It took an effort, but she remained calm and her smile never faltered.

She looked across the table to her younger son, resplendent in evening dress. Good manners also prevented him from flinching when Monique touched his arm and looked him over seductively, flirting outrageously.

He proposed a toast to the newlywed couple with dignity and warmth, wishing them health and happiness and welcoming David's wife to the Tracklin family. The guests raised their wine glasses to toast the happy couple.

That he found the woman crude and boorish was a secret known only to himself.

The picture of a woman with soft brown eyes and dark curly hair filled his memory; graceful, poised and gentle, no dyed hair with dark roots, false eyelashes and rouged face. The scent of her was fresh and floral, not cloying like the potent perfume Monique favored. She didn't try to impress or draw attention to herself.

Julie's simple sweetness would be trampled on by women like Monique. Nasty comments and harsh criticism would wound her, not go over her head as they did with David's wife. She lived in a different world, far from this false glamour, fake friendliness and deceit.

He missed that world.

He must think of some plausible reason to return to Desolation Sound. It was such a tiny part of the Tracklin enterprise, but surely the threat of a strike was good reason to keep a close watch on it, no matter how small the profits compared to the entire company. He must go back—it was a sane place where people had their feet on the ground and didn't pretend to be something they were not.

His manners were impeccable; he dutifully danced with his sister-in-law and all the elderly relatives who gushed over him.

"How handsome you've grown. Why I remember when you were just a little boy. How quickly time passes."

Andrew smiled and murmured polite responses, all the while thinking of fresh breezes, clean air and a sailing companion with a lilting voice and a soothing manner that made him want to escape the confines of this stuffy, polite society as soon as he possibly could.

Before this evening, he had never felt the difficulty of being a Tracklin son. His gaze settled on his brother David, completely besotted with his new wife, seeing none of the things he found so irritating. He felt sympathy for David—too much responsibility too soon, no wonder he was willing to abandon it for the first woman who lured him out of the office. He feared David had made a terrible mistake . . . but hoped he was wrong.

"Andrew," an insistent female voice called. "You've been avoiding me. Where have you been these past weeks?"

The tall, slender woman kissed him with the familiarity of an old friend. She was dressed in the height of fashion and dripped with expensive jewelry. She attached herself to Andrew's arm with a possessiveness he didn't encourage.

"Nicole, you're looking lovely, as usual."

The words were what she wanted to hear, but Andrew Tracklin had said them in such a way they seemed almost insulting. Her bottom lip protruded slightly, a pout that anyone who knew Nikki Ashton realized she wasn't getting her own way.

She looked up at him coyly through darkly mascaraed lashes. "Now that David is married, you are the most eligible bachelor in town. You'll have to marry soon, darling—a suitable wife—someone like me."

Andrew Tracklin raised his eyebrows and gave Nikki Ashton a scorching look. But she wasn't deterred.

"We've known each other forever, our mothers are best friends, and I know all the right people. We're perfect for each other." She gave him that simpering look and he choked back vicious words that would rid her of any such idea.

He thought of Nikki Ashton dressed in nautical fashion, sipping champagne on the decks of millionaires' yachts. She loved the moneyed lifestyle but he knew she turned green with nausea at the mention of casting off from the yacht club dock. Her glamorous exterior was all for show; the person beneath was shallow and mean-spirited, unlike a natural beauty who kept invading his thoughts. There was nothing false about *her*. Nikki Ashton paled in comparison.

He appeared the perfect gentleman, but his tightly clenched fists betrayed strong emotions held in check. "I'm afraid I'm much too old and set in my ways for you, Nicole."

"Don't be silly, Andrew. You're not that old; what you need is a wife and an active social life."

The social life Nikki Ashton led made him shudder. The last thing he wanted was to be dragged from one fashion show to another, from one expensive nightclub to the next, or from one boring dinner party with 'the right people' to another.

"Indeed." His quiet voice was deceptive.

"Where have you been hiding yourself? Your secretary refuses to put my calls through and you don't answer the messages I leave at your townhouse." She said this in a little-girl voice he might have found cute long ago, but tonight he found it extremely annoying.

"I have a business to run, Nicole."

Seeing no softening in his icy-blue eyes, Nikki Ashton giggled seductively. "Oh, Andrew, you've turned into a stick-in-the-mud. You're so serious."

The cajoling tone didn't impress him. He stood elegantly tall, splendidly dressed; the picture of good breeding and fine manners, but no glimmer of warmth was there in the icy sparkle of his eyes or in the frostiness of his voice.

Any woman less conceited or wrapped up in herself would have noticed and scurried away in rejection. But not Nikki Ashton.

"You simply have to take me out, Andrew. There's a dance at the yacht club Saturday. You can pick me up at seven o'clock—"

"I'm afraid not, Nicole," he cut her off. "I'll be out of town next weekend." This was the first he knew of it himself, but he planned to be at Desolation Sound by Saturday.

"Then I expect to hear from you as soon as you get back." She flounced off across the ballroom with an exaggerated sway of her hips, girlishly flirting with the next most eligible bachelor in the room.

Much later, a weary Andrew Tracklin stood beside his parents as they bid good night to the last of the departing guests.

"That went rather well, don't you think?" Rebecca Tracklin commented to no one in particular.

"A fine welcome to our newest family member."

"Do you really think so, dear?"

"Better than she deserves," her husband growled. "All your care and attention, fine food and excellent champagne was wasted on that young woman. Hamburgers at Mc-Donald's would suit her."

"Robert! Shame on you! She's our daughter-in-law now and deserves our respect."

Her husband grunted, knowing she was correct but unwilling to agree. He loosened his tie, unbuttoned his vest, and quickly changed the subject.

"Have you tied up all the loose ends on Desolation Sound?"

"Everything is taken care of. David had big plans but I found them premature. Expansion and mechanization aren't wise at this time, neither is chemical spraying."

"I wondered about that. David was so sure."

"I forestalled any rash actions. We received an intelligent plea to curtail spraying. The board has put things on hold pending further investigation." He thought about it for a moment. "I never did find out exactly who authored that well-put piece of wisdom. The board traced him to Northern Chemicals, but he's not available for meetings until next month." He looked at his father, a man who worked long years in the forest industry. "Have you ever run across a chemist by the name of Marantse?"

The senior Mr. Tracklin pondered the name. "Can't say I know any chemist by that name. The name sounds familiar . . . aah, I remember . . . won the Swiftsure two years in a row . . . marvelous sailors."

Andrew Tracklin was distracted by his mother. "You two, stop talking business. It's late and we deserve a final brandy before we go to our beds. Business can wait till morning."

The two men agreed and moved into the study to pour the brandy.

They toasted David's and Monique's happiness once more, each keeping their personal opinions of the new Mrs. Tracklin to themselves, then retired to their beds. Proprieties observed, a job well done.

Rampant trailing cucumber vines spread their leafy tendrils across the entire bottom of the garden. First, small yellow flowers, then tiny cucumbers and now, this morning, bushels of straight green cucumbers at the perfect stage for dill pickles. Julie picked all of them before they had a chance to become huge, yellow, and seedy—only good for relish. She scrubbed them in the water trough and gathered bunches of fragrant dill. She had dug up garlic bulbs the previous day and braided them to hang in the hot sun. With a braid of garlic added to her armload of dill, she carried the cucumbers to the house.

Anna sang as she heated the canning kettle and sterilized jars. The kitchen smelled of vinegar, brine and spices, and echoed with Anna's pure, clear voice. She smiled as Julie lugged in the bushel basket of washed cucumbers.

"Splendid crop. Last year it rained so much, our cucumbers rotted with mildew before they ripened."

"Looks like enough here for five years' worth of dill pickles."

Anna started packing the jars, first a stalk of dill, then some garlic, a bay leaf, and finally the cucumbers, tightly packed and ready for the hot vinegar and brine. "Remember Grandmother saying, 'The winter is long?' She put up hundreds of jars of fruit, pickles and relish."

"I remember—a never-ending job. I'll take the fresh produce section at a supermarket any day." As quickly as Anna filled the jars, she added lids and processed them, timing them carefully, then setting them to cool and immediately filling the canner with the next lot.

The two sisters worked steadily together. The mountain of cucumbers was turned into dill pickles in much less time than Julie expected.

"Did you have a good sail up the sound with Andrew Tracklin?"

"Super."

"Have you told him about yourself yet?"

"I told him about sailing with Grandfather and our parents' divorce . . . stuff like that."

"And . . . ?"

Julie gave her sister a vexed look. "And . . . what?"

"And, what else? I'm sure he wants to know more about you."

"You've lived in the woods too long, Anna. We enjoyed sailing but our time together is limited. We'll both be moving on soon."

"Julie, he can't overlook the fact that you're educated and bright."

"Men don't notice things like that."

Anna put her hands on her hips and gave Julie a scolding look.

"It's true, Anna."

Anna let out a loud groan. "I think Andrew Tracklin notices—he's just too polite to ask a lot of questions."

"He'd ask if he wanted to know."

"Don't you think you should tell him? It's dishonest. You can't go on pretending to be some naive waif fresh from the backwoods."

"Anna, it doesn't matter. No harm is done. I haven't actually lied . . . some things just haven't been discussed. Anyway, our paths will never cross once I leave Desolation Sound. Ours is an encounter with no future."

"I'm not so sure about that."

"Take my word for it. You've seen the man—anyone who looks like that has women swarming around him like bees to honey. A brief encounter with me doesn't get a second thought."

"But Julie . . ."

She stretched her arms wide. "Look at me, Anna. I'm as brown as old leather, scratched from the cucumber vines, barefoot, and wearing clothes so shabby the Goodwill wouldn't accept them. The sophisticated Mr. Tracklin would be appalled."

"He didn't look appalled to me."

"Anna, you're impossible! You've been away from people for too long. Forget the man." She gestured to the rows of filled jars on the table. "Let's get all this canning put away."

With Daniel's help, they carried the quart jars of dill pickles down to the root cellar to join the shelves of canned fruit, vegetables, jams and juice stored away for the winter. A sense of pride and contentment filled all three as they took stock of the winter's provisions.

Julie was very wrong. Andrew Tracklin thought a great deal about her. His meeting with government officials to discuss their forest practices code took up much of the week. They adjourned on Friday to resume talks Monday morning.

With some clever organizing and a briefcase full of papers to study, he was on the first ferry to Powell River early Saturday. He had the excuse of leaving Daniel Corwin stranded on Desolation Sound with his boat at dock in Powell River. As Andrew was responsible for the situation, he was obligated to get Daniel back to his boat. Who knew when the Corwins might have an emergency that required immediate transportation?

And, of course, it would give him a chance to talk with Julie, that is, if he could get her alone for any length of time. That woman was a blur of motion, always some work demanding her attention and never a quiet moment without the children or her sister and brother-in-law. If he could get her away from Desolation Sound . . .

Three solid days of relentless rain kept the Corwin household cooped up indoors. The dark gray banks of cloud hung low over the water, blocking out the distant islands, any passing boats, and even the sea itself.

A heavy mist engulfed Desolation Sound, dripping wet and shivery. Raindrops plopped off the eaves and trickled in little streams across rocks to the sea. Gardening had come to a standstill and Julie's outdoor chores were made difficult by the constant deluge of water, making the ground slippery mud underfoot. Geraldine refused to leave her dry shed and even the chickens stayed in their coop rather than scratch around in the downpour.

She read to the children, taught them card games they didn't already know, cleaned the house till it shone, and tried every new recipe in Anna's cookbook they had ingredients for. Still, Julie was restless.

To her delight, Anna discovered she could hold a paintbrush again for long hours, and returned to her unfinished canvas, completely engrossed in her painting, barely answering when spoken to, and oblivious to the sopping rain outside the large windows of the studio. She was thrilled to regain the use of her arm and lost all track of time as she mixed her oil paints and painted with the enthusiasm forced dormant these past months.

Daniel, too, had picked up his paintbrushes. His delicate watercolors captured the beauty of the landscape with trees, wildflowers and sea birds, light and blending into the paint-washed sky. Daniel's paintings were small in size and looked simple and quickly dashed off, but their lack of adornment required intricate balance and perfect use of color—an arduous task of great patience. The result was a painting that looked effortless—very different from Anna's bright portraits and large canvasses.

Simon happily played with his building blocks, but Jake and Moira were fidgeting with the lack of activity; like caged animals they paced and restlessly discarded one distraction after another, teasing each other and squabbling over the tiniest things.

"Have you ever camped overnight in the forest?" Julie thought a nice hike, a chance to stretch their legs, and a hearty meal cooked over the campfire would break this waterlogged boredom.

"No. Simon is still too little." Jake's eyes lit up with enthusiasm. "We could go, couldn't we, Julie?"

"As soon as the rain stops."

Moira and Jake wriggled with excitement at the thought of overnight camping. "I could get the tent out from the loft," Jake offered. "And we have sleeping bags. What else do we need, Julie?"

"A first aid kit, a compass and some food . . . rain gear."

"I'll help pack food," Moira volunteered. "Dad has a little camp stove."

The rest of the afternoon was spent packing gear, making grand plans, and anxiously glancing out the rain-streaked windows at the endless miserable weather.

"The wind is down," Jake observed hopefully, "and I'm sure the rain is easing off."

An hour later, he added, "The fog is lifting. I see a clear patch."

The frequent weather observations, updated every few minutes, finally gave encouragement. "There's a patch of blue to the west. The rain is definitely stopping. Tomorrow has to be sunny."

It was true; the rain did stop that evening. After dinner, Jake and Moira willingly washed and got ready for bed without being asked. "We'll have to be up early to get a good start, won't we Julie?"

She couldn't disappoint such eagerness. "Right after breakfast," she promised. "If the rain holds off."

Saturday morning dawned clear and bright, the sun sizzling clouds of steam off the wet roofs and ground. Daniel offered to do everyone's morning chores so the keen hikers could eat a full breakfast and set off boldly into the woods, bursting with unspent energy after three days cooped up indoors.

Daniel, Anna and Simon waved to the intrepid backpackers as they set off along the trail, into the trees densely covering the hillside. Julie was as keen to stretch her legs as Jake and Moira. She would be deeply missed by the

Corwin family when she returned to Vancouver, and that day was not far off now.

Guessing her husband's thoughts, Anna squeezed his hand. "She's a treasure, isn't she?"

He smiled and nodded. His sister-in-law had added sparkle to all their lives. He watched her heading off at a brisk pace with his two eldest children, then turned back to Anna. "I'm rather fond of her older sister too."

They shared a hug, then headed for the barn.

Morning chores took longer without Julie. Geraldine allowed Anna to milk her, but not without some sidestepping and noisy bleating. Anna's leg was still a little stiff but she managed to milk the goat; her arm was almost back to normal.

Daniel and Simon carried in wood, pumped water, gathered eggs, and rejoiced in the chance to be outside again.

From his helicopter, Andrew Tracklin spotted Daniel and Simon by the water pump as he landed in the clearing. There was no sign of the curly-haired woman wearing skimpy shorts anywhere in the yard. She must be inside cooking something delicious for lunch.

But she wasn't there. The sun was bright, yet it felt as if a cloud had thrown its light in shadow.

"Where is the rest of your family?" he casually asked Anna, the urgency in his tone not escaping her notice.

"They're hiking into the forest to camp overnight. After three days of endless rain . . . they needed exercise." Her gentle smile gave no hint of how restless and irritable children could get in cramped quarters. He didn't need to be told; he was restless himself.

"The promise of adventure was so enticing, it was hard to convince them to stay out only one night. With Julie carrying most of the supplies, another day's provisions would've broken her back. She's strong . . . but she's not a packhorse."

Daniel laughed. "Julie wasn't complaining; she was as

keen to climb the hill as Jake and Moira. This endless rain
has gotten to everyone."

The expression on Andrew Tracklin's face prompted him
to add, "They're in no danger. Julie's an experienced hiker,
sensible too. The children will have a great time." Andrew's furrowed brow and look of doubt, left Daniel puzzled. He didn't look at all pleased about the camping
expedition.

It wasn't the children Andrew was concerned about.

He brought his attention back to the two people staring
at him. He smiled and said, "I was in Powell River and
saw your boat still at dock there. If I take you to it by
helicopter, would you like to sail it around to Desolation
Sound this afternoon? I feel responsible for leaving you
stranded without it."

Daniel stroked his whiskered chin. "I was beginning to
wonder about that." He looked at Anna. "Will you be all
right alone here with Simon?"

"I'll be fine. I'm good as new, a little gimpy, but Simon's
here to help."

The little boy grinned from ear to ear.

"It's settled then. Is there anything you'd like from Powell River?"

"No. We'll make a trip in for winter provisions later in
the month."

Anna noticed Andrew Tracklin's reluctance. If he returned Daniel to his boat, he'd have no excuse for his frequent visits to the Corwin home.

"Will you be staying on in Powell River?"

"No, only for the weekend. I have meetings with government officials Monday."

She couldn't resist adding, "Jake and Moira and Julie
will be sorry to have missed you."

A cloud passed over those vivid blue eyes. "I'm sorry to
have missed them too."

Anna knew it! He wasn't letting on, but he wanted to see Julie . . . she just knew.

But her husband had no such thoughts. "Let's get moving," Daniel urged. "If we leave now, I can bring the boat around before dark."

Nothing more was said, but Andrew's disappointment was visible in his sad eyes and the droop of his shoulders.

The helicopter lifted easily from the pasture, but instead of rising quickly and disappearing out of sight over the hilltop, it circled the hillside, looking for any signs of three hikers in the woods. One brief look was all he needed.

Jake's bright yellow jacket glinted out from beneath a stand of cedars. On closer inspection, Moira's red sweater and Julie's orange backpack were also clearly visible. They had covered a lot of distance since leaving this morning.

The three hikers moved out from under the tree cover and waved at the Tracklin helicopter. It was only then that it dipped to the south and cleared the hill, heading for Powell River.

The pilot looked straight ahead, into the misty clouds.

He'd been denied the chance to be alone with her once again, to ask all the questions and fill in all the blanks.

Maybe it was for the best. No sense prolonging the pain.

It would be like throwing a lamb to the wolves, expecting Julie to hold her own with the likes of Monique and Nikki Ashton.

Her happiness was down there on that forested hillside.

"You should've seen it, Dad. It was this big! The fattest raccoon ever, and mean too."

"She had three babies," Moira added. "Julie said they were after our chocolate. It's a good thing we hung our food from that tree."

"We made bannock bread over the fire like Indians did. It was excellent!"

"Mr. Tracklin visited while you were off adventuring."

"Yeah, we saw the helicopter."

"He took your father to bring our boat back and pick up our mail." The children hushed, all eyes on their mother, suspecting something special.

"Now that I'm in good health, and while Julie is still here to look after Geraldine and the chickens, your grandparents have invited us to stay with them for a week in Parksville."

Only Moira frowned at the phrase, 'while Julie is *still* here.' She loved her aunt and didn't want her to leave. Jake and Simon were too excited to notice—a trip to Daniel's parents, driving in their car, going to the movies, eating ice cream—all the treats missing on Desolation Sound. They could hardly wait.

"When, Dad?"

"In ten days' time. I want to haul the boat up and scrape the bottom before taking her across to Parksville."

"Whoopee! What should we do first, Moira?"

"Grandpa promised to teach me to ride a bicycle. Do you think one week is enough time?"

Catching Anna's cunning wink, Julie saw her sister's devious mind at work. With the excitement of visiting their grandparents, the children would be distracted, and Julie could slip away home without prolonged tears, whining and sadness.

"If the land is flat and there's pavement to practice on, one week should do the trick."

"Do you think so, Julie? It's very flat by Grandpa's house."

"I know so, Moira. You'll be able to cycle round the sea wall in Stanley Park with me next time you come to visit." That planted the idea that Julie would soon be going home. *So far, so good.*

"TV," Simon remembered. "Big Bird."

"We have work before we go. Any offers to help get the boat ready?"

All three children dashed down to the dock with Daniel, skipping gleefully and all talking at once. Things were back to normal.

"Andrew was disappointed you weren't here when he came."

"Honestly, Anna. Is that what he said?"

"Not exactly ... well, not in those words ... but he looked so let down. I knew he wanted to see you."

"Stick to the facts, Anna. What were his exact words?"

Anna shifted her weight from one foot to the other and looked past Julie to the children on the dock. Julie wouldn't let her evade the question. "Okay, stick-to-the-facts scientist! He said he was sorry to have missed you. But I know he meant much more than that."

Julie looked thoughtful.

"It *was* something more, Julie. Andrew was disappointed. He wanted to see you, I just know he did."

"He came to fly Daniel to Powell River."

"That was his excuse, really, he wanted to see you ..."

Julie grinned. "It'll do your imagination good to get away for a few days. Soon you'll believe you can read minds and the entrails of chickens!"

The two sisters laughed and continued on down to the dock. Anna wanted to take photographs to share with her in-laws and there was a painting in her mind's eye demanding to be put on canvas. It required photographs of Julie standing at the end of the dock looking out to sea. She could see it now—a wistful expression, a longing for something gone away, a background of distant islands, calm sea and cloud-streaked sky.

This place was so gorgeous! She couldn't paint it enough times.

Mrs. Wyatt placed the typed letters, ready for signing, on Mr. Tracklin's desk. The man worked like a Trojan, more productive than his brother, as intelligent and clear thinking as his father, but with more knowledge of government procedures and the need for public relations.

She'd known Andrew Tracklin since he was a young lad visiting his father's office. He'd changed lately; driving himself, in the office before she arrived in the morning, and from the prolific amount of work accomplished, still in the office when she went to bed at night.

"Did you want to say something, Mrs. Wyatt?"

"You mustn't take this wrong, sir. I've worked for your father twenty-five years and known you as a boy. I mean no disrespect."

"What is it, Mrs. Wyatt?"

"Sending flowers often helps, sir—a nice bouquet and a little card."

Andrew Tracklin set his pen down and stared at his father's secretary. "Sending flowers?"

"Yes, sir. It lets a woman know you care. I can see the signs you've quarreled; you're touchy, you snap at people ... it would make life easier for the whole office if you'd make up with her. Send her a nice bouquet, sir. See if it doesn't work."

His grim expression softened, traces of a smile creased the edges of his mouth. "It's more complicated than that, Mrs. Wyatt."

"Nothing's ever so complicated a few kind words can't straighten it out. Pick up the telephone and talk to her. See if I'm not right."

"I can't reach her by telephone."

"Then you'll have to go to her. You're driving yourself to an early grave, sulking about the way you are."

"Sulking?"

"Yes, sulking!" A shrewd pair of eyes stared over glasses perched on her nose. "Take my advice. You have a meeting in Victoria Wednesday that can't be avoided; but give yourself a break tomorrow and go talk to her." She turned and walked to the door.

She was stopped before her hand grasped the handle. "Mrs. Wyatt."

The steel in that deep voice had her wondering if her job of twenty-five years was over.

She looked back at her boss. He smiled, a little sheepishly.

"Thanks."

Chapter Seven

"Stand still, Julie."

"Anna, I'm stiff all over, my nose is itchy, I have to sneeze, and you've been looking at me all twenty-eight years of my life—you must be able to paint me with your eyes closed by now."

"Just a few more minutes. The light is perfect."

The clatter of helicopter blades sliced through the gentle lapping of waves against the dock, shattering the silence and breaking Anna's concentration.

"Okay. Enough for today. I wanted to get more done, but that helicopter's brought you a reprieve. You're the worst subject for painting; you never keep still."

Julie rotated her shoulders and stretched her arms, shaking flexibility back into her rigid limbs. She was stiff all over from inactivity.

"Help me carry my easel back up to the house. It looks like we're going to have a visitor."

Julie never thought she'd be so glad to see that green and white Tracklin helicopter. Posing for one of Anna's paintings was hard work; keeping still, no fidgeting. She welcomed being distracted by a blue-eyed pilot who swooped down out of the sky. He came at the exact time she most wanted to see him (truth was, she wanted to see him almost all the time). While Anna organized her paints and canvas, Julie picked up the easel and stool, balanced them in her arms, and puffed up the incline to the house.

Andrew Tracklin strolled across the pasture, eyes riveted on the dark-haired woman in skimpy shorts and a tattered T-shirt that clung in all the right places. He, on the other hand, looked as though he'd come directly from his office; clean-shaven, spotless, the height of men's fashion. Only his suit jacket had been discarded, all the better to see his pale blue shirt and darker blue tie; the man knew how to dress. Did he have any idea how glorious he looked? Those blue eyes of his were vibrant, accentuated by the blue of his shirt and tie and fixed on the woman struggling with the easel.

Out of breath, Julie flushed as she watched him draw near. Her heart was racing—the awkward easel must be heavier than she thought.

He didn't give her a chance to argue, merely walked up to her and reached for the load she almost dropped at the sound of his voice.

"Allow me." She hadn't remembered how deep his voice was . . . or how good he smelled.

"Thanks," she mumbled.

He couldn't resist—he gently kissed the back of her neck as he reached around to take the easel out of her arms as if it weighed no more than a feather. Julie blushed, aware that Anna could see them from the dock. She could just imagine her sister grinning and saying, "I told you so." She stumbled, but regained her footing and carried Anna's stool the remaining distance to the house.

Andrew stood holding the door open for her. "Have you been painting?"

"Oh, no. Not me. Drawing a straight line is a challenge for me. Anna is the artist in the family."

His smile was gentle, but the way his eyes drank in the

sight of her was unsettling. Julie bent her head to avoid his gaze and led the way through to Anna's studio. "You can put the easel down beside the window." When she raised her eyes to look at him, she dropped the stool and it clattered to the floor.

She took a deep breath—she was so light-headed, awestruck being close to this Greek god of a man. She was behaving like Jake when Andrew first dropped down in the bramble patch. She pulled back her shoulders and stiffened her spine. My, but the man was handsome.

The walls splendidly covered with masterpieces in both watercolors and oils didn't catch his attention. He saw none of them.

She was everything he'd remembered—fresh, tanned, vibrantly alive, innocently beautiful . . . everything Nicole Ashton was not. His mind hadn't been playing tricks on him.

The silence between them lengthened, as though speaking would break the magic spell and both of them would disappear up in smoke.

Unaware of the tension building in her studio, Anna limped in with her paint box and brushes.

"Andrew, how nice to see you again." She took him by the arm and was leading him to the kitchen. "Come join us for tea."

Julie relaxed. Her imagination had gotten the better of her there, for a moment, but Anna brought her back to reality with a thump.

Daniel and the children burst into the kitchen like fireworks exploding with words. Julie was able to fade into the background, slice sandwiches and put the kettle on for tea.

"We're going to our grandparents."

"Did you see that plush yacht in the Sound? We heard it's some famous Hollywood movie star on a fishing trip."

"Can we see inside your helicopter again?"

"One at a time, children," Anna's calming voice broke in. "Give Mr. Tracklin a chance to catch his breath." She winked at Julie. She *had* seen that kiss on the way to the house.

He was breathless, all right, but it had nothing to do with the three children gathered around him, all talking at once.

He stood tall, straightened his tie, and smiled at the children with a warm indulgence that reminded Julie of her grandfather. "I have something for you in my helicopter. If you want to look inside it once more, let's go now, shall we?"

He was swept out the door by six clutching hands, three ecstatic voices and six urgent feet, setting off at a run. There was so little chance to be alone with Julie.

Anna stood beside Julie, helping to prepare a special tea. "Told you so."

"Told me so, what?"

"Told you he wanted to see you."

"Anna Corwin, you're daft! He just raced out the door."

Anna gave her sister a smug look as they carried cups and plates to the table. "You'll see."

Julie saw nothing. The children were back and Andrew was carrying a huge, cellophane-wrapped gift basket of tropical fruit—pineapple, bananas, papayas, mangoes and some other things she didn't recognize, tied with a giant red bow. It was magnificent.

It wasn't the bouquet of flowers Mrs. Wyatt had suggested. When he looked at those refrigerated blooms in the florist's shop, they seemed so cold and forced, artificial, even though they were fresh. They weren't what he wanted to give to Julie—there was nothing artificial or forced about her, nothing cold or refrigerated either. She was wild and free and delightfully beautiful just as she was, not arranged, clipped and tightly fitted into some confining vase. The exotic fruit seemed something she'd enjoy more . . . and be able to share. She did have a generous nature. He wasn't disappointed.

"Is that a pineapple?"

"Yes, silly. Remember we saw pictures in a book about Hawaii?"

"What are those fuzzy brown things?"

"Kiwis."

"Can we eat them?"

Daniel produced a paring knife and sliced a kiwi for his children to sample.

"It's pretty," Moira observed, not too sure about biting into anything so green in color.

"Tastes good," Simon encouraged her.

Anna was obviously pleased. "Thank you, Andrew. This *is* a treat."

"We could be eating stuff like this on a South Sea island, couldn't we, Dad?"

"Yes, son. We could." Daniel's full beard hid his smile, but his hazel eyes spoke volumes. "Very kind of you, Tracklin."

All talking stopped as the happy group tucked into tea, sandwiches and the tropical fruit. It was a wonderful change from the small fruits and berries that could be grown on Desolation Sound. The beaming faces around the table were gratifying, but Julie's beautiful smile was his reward. "Thank you," she said, looking him full in the face. "I've been craving oranges for months."

"I'm glad you approve."

Andrew wondered how best to bring up the invitation he'd rehearsed but found no opportunity to make.

He cleared his throat.

"I'll be in Victoria for the day tomorrow. Is there anything you need from the city?"

Anna was the first to respond. "I need oil paints, there's a great art supply shop on Fort Street. I need canvasses too.

Julie, you know the kind I mean. No one has them in Powell River."

He could have blessed Anna; this was the opening he'd waited for. Looking at Julie with all his held-back emotion under control, he asked as though it was of little concern to him, "Would you like to spend the day in Victoria, visit the shops, see the sights? It would be no inconvenience. Tracklin's has a suite at The Empress, you could stay there overnight and I'd fly you back Wednesday evening."

Julie was leaving Desolation Sound for good soon; this was a fine way for the Corwins to get back to normal without her constant presence. It would be a first step to make that final break less difficult. They'd come to depend on her so much these past months. And she'd love to have some time alone with Andrew; maybe they could finally finish a conversation without being interrupted.

She searched the dear faces around the table for any objections. Everyone seemed happy to see her go for the day. Anna showed no sign of wanting to shop for art supplies herself.

"Great idea. Julie, you've been isolated here so long you've forgotten what a city is like. Don't worry about me; I'm getting stronger every day . . . and Daniel's here if I get into trouble." It was almost as though Anna had planned the whole thing with Andrew Tracklin.

That didn't leave any chance to refuse. She looked into those intense blue eyes and smiled. "Thank you for the offer. I'd enjoy a day in Victoria."

He swallowed quickly, hardly believing his luck. He gave no outward sign. He didn't want to scare her off. He was cheering on the inside but remained calm, appearing distant and unconcerned.

"I'd like to leave as soon as possible, settle in at The Empress and go over a sheath of papers before tomorrow's meeting."

Julie got the hint; the invitation wasn't going to be repeated. Quickly she was up out of her chair, ready to change into the only possible clothing suitable—the same pink sweater and long skirt.

She turned to the Corwins still seated around the table. "Each of you make a wish list and I'll try to find at least one thing for everyone." In the scramble for paper and pencils, she dashed off to change and find her purse, pushed to the back of a drawer the day she arrived. She hadn't much cash but her ATM card and Visa card would cover any expenses.

With Anna's help, Jake and Moira spelled out the items for their list—a Swiss army knife and a hair barrette. Daniel helped Simon by printing his dearest wish—a picture book about a tugboat.

Andrew tried not to reveal his triumphant feelings about getting Julie alone at last. He helped clear the dishes and wipe the table as he'd seen her do many times. She was back in a flash with a shoulder bag holding all she would need for an overnight stay, looking fresh and exuberant in that delightful sweater and skirt. She moved with a feminine grace and self-confidence—not unlike the woman he'd last glimpsed hiking all over the hillside with two excited children.

Her tanned face glowed with vitality and her soft brown eyes sparkled. "Give me your lists; I'll do my best to fill them."

Amidst hugs and kisses and whispered requests, Julie left the Corwin house to walk across the clearing to the helicopter with a tall strong man beside her, a quivery feeling inside her, knowing she would soon be leaving those five people so dear to her for more than just one day. His arm across her shoulders was reassuring.

They flew directly to Pat Bay Airport, then took a taxi to The Empress Hotel.

The streetlights flashing by, traffic on the road, cars honking, and the sights and sounds of city living surrounded Julie like old familiar friends she had missed these past months but hadn't realized how much, until she saw them again.

Her companion saw her alert eyes taking in every small movement, her awareness of each passing car, intruding sound and bright light.

"Have you been to Victoria before?'

"Yes, several years ago, though. After life on Desolation Sound, I forgot how noisy a city could be." She swept her hands to encompass the inner harbor and brightly lit Parliament Buildings. "It's a shock to the system after only the light of an oil lamp, the chirping of birds, and the single clatter of one helicopter."

He grimaced slightly at that reference to his noisy intrusion into her quiet life. "Is city life that terrible?"

"Oh no. I like the people, the bright lights, the entertainment." She looked at his skeptical expression. "Don't get me wrong . . . I like rural life too . . . and the silence of drifting at sea with no one else in sight." She shrugged. "I like it all."

He laughed. She embraced life with enthusiasm. He wondered if living in a large city would change her, but before he got the chance to inquire further, the taxi pulled up at the entrance to The Empress and the driver was holding the door open for them.

Andrew was surprised to see how natural Julie seemed walking across the stately lobby, relaxed and poised, not in the least intimidated by her luxurious surroundings. He guided her to the elevators with his hand at her back, overwhelmed by an urge to protect her and keep her natural beauty untainted.

The Tracklin suite was elegant; antique pieces, plush carpets, fine oil paintings—reflecting his parents' taste. Julie didn't gaze in awe at the fine furnishings, the remarkable view of the inner harbor, or the spaciousness of the vast bedroom he showed her. Her eyes zeroed in on the CD player in the sitting room and the collection of classical music. Ignoring her palatial surroundings, she scanned the CD titles with unconcealed delight, like a child on Christmas morning.

"You enjoy classical music?"

"Oh yes. This is a splendid collection." She paused, hesitant to be handling someone's prized cache of CDs. She looked down at her hands, clutching a recording by the New York Philharmonic.

"Don't look so guilty. You're welcome to listen to as many as you like. It's my mother's collection and she'd be thrilled to share it with another music lover. She seldom meets anyone as enthusiastic as herself."

The huge smile that lit her face as she flipped through the CD collection stopped him from suggesting they might tour the city, stop at some popular nightspots. Little by little, he was learning more about this woman. *She liked classical music:* He made a mental note, another piece to the puzzle.

"Shall I order us something from room service?"

"Not for me." She looked at him with those soulful brown eyes, almost bashfully if he wasn't mistaken. He guessed she had something to ask but was holding back. He was looking forward to spending this evening with her.

"Okay. Out with it. What's behind that look?"

"I saw the most glorious bathroom, with running hot water and a bathtub to drown in . . . you go ahead and order from room service . . . but . . . would you be insulted if I soaked in a hot tub and used gallons of hot water to wash the wood smoke out of my hair and scrub away all the soot and cedar bits clinging to me? It's been so long since I've been near a huge, deep bathtub."

This was not what he had planned. "A woman turning down my invitation to sip wine and nibble small delicacies?" He dramatically put his hand over his heart. "I'm crushed."

Julie laughed and he joined in. "I understand the lure of modern conveniences." He gestured toward the guest bedroom. "Be my guest."

Julie turned toward the bedroom. Another huge bedroom was on the other side of the sitting room; she wondered if it also had a bathroom of its own.

She glanced back at the man looking so thoughtful, standing watching her. "I won't be hogging the only bathroom, will I?"

"No. There's another one off the master suite."

He didn't mention it had a Jacuzzi and he'd love to share it with her. It was too soon to spring such thoughts on her. He didn't want to spoil her fun. "Enjoy your soak."

"Thanks. I'll leave you free to study your reports for tomorrow's meeting." She disappeared into the guest room, softly closing the door behind her.

This wasn't how he'd expected the evening to go. Nothing about this woman was what he expected. Instead of being thrilled by the prospect of his company, wining and dining, dancing and sampling the city's nightlife, she was ecstatic over the sight of a CD player and chose a solitary bath.

He poured himself a glass of sherry and opened his briefcase. She was right; he had to prepare for tomorrow. This wasn't going to be the romantic evening he'd envisioned . . . but he'd be well informed for tomorrow's discussions. With a sigh, he picked up the first of his reports.

After nearly an hour of shampooing her tangled hair, soaking in a scented bubble bath, filing her jagged nails, and putting lotion on her chapped hands, knees, and elbows, Julie slipped on her old pajamas and borrowed the terry cloth robe hanging on the bathroom door.

She hadn't heard a sound from the rest of the suite. Perhaps Andrew had gone out and she could listen to music for a while without disturbing him. It had been so long since she experienced the joy of a good sound system—

Anna's singing voice was great but . . . She opened her bed-room door cautiously, to be instantly greeted by a deep male voice.

"Enjoy your bath?"

Julie stepped into the sitting room, now softly lit by table lamps, her bare feet sinking into the deep-pile carpet.

"Yes, thank you." She felt suddenly shy.

She hadn't expected to see her host sitting casually on the sofa, hair wet from his shower, dressed in a terry cloth robe similar to the one she had on, only much bigger. He patted the sofa cushion beside him.

"Come join me. I took the liberty of ordering you some-thing."

Julie noticed the sherry glass in his hand and looked down at the tray on the low mahogany table in front of him. As she cautiously sat, he lifted the cloth covering the tray.

"Milk and cookies, or in this case, hot chocolate and cookies."

She didn't know if he was making fun of her for being as unsophisticated as a child . . . but she didn't care . . . the hot chocolate had a dollop of whipped cream on top and smelled wonderful . . . and she was hungry. "This looks lovely."

Her hesitant smile pleased him. He passed her the hot mug. "Now tell me, which piece of music would you like to hear first?"

There was no hesitation in her response. *"The Water Music Suite.* I saw an arrangement there by Eugene Ormandy and the Philadelphia Orchestra."

"A woman who knows her own mind." He slipped the CD into the player, then resumed his seat beside her on the sofa, his head back against the cushions and his feet resting on the low table before them. The first strains of music filled the room. Julie leaned back sipping her hot chocolate, her legs tucked up under her, absorbed in the music, unaware of the arm across the back of the sofa or the attentive blue eyes absorbing her presence.

When her drink was finished, she placed the empty mug on the tray and snuggled back against the arm that had drawn her into Andrew's side and held her there as they listened to the music, without speaking, each peacefully content, and free of any need for idle comments or nervous chatter.

Now would be a good time to tell him about her work and her life in Vancouver—but she was so comfortable, sleepy and relaxed after her hot bath, unwilling to break the spell of the beautiful music.

Andrew didn't want to break the spell, either. This woman was restful to be with; she recharged his spirits, filled him with new energy. Sitting here in bathrobes listening to music, no makeup or fancy dress, no expensive nightclub or crowds of people—his old flight crew would be surprised. For that matter, he was surprised. He inhaled the lingering fragrance of shampoo and bubble bath and relaxed into the sofa, Julie warm and drowsy beside him.

The music finished and Julie sighed, nestling into the warm folds of Andrew's bathrobe. He kissed the top of her curly head.

"You're a soothing person to be with."

Julie lifted her chin, eyelids half shut and voice husky with sleepiness. "Is that a polite way of saying I'm boring?"

He looked down at her sleepy face. "Never boring, Julie, never boring."

She rested her cheek back on his chest. "Hmm," she murmured.

"Tell me about yourself. What happens when you leave Corwin's?"

"I go back to my own home."

"Where do you live?"

"In town."

"What do you do there?"

"I work for a living." Julie took a deep breath and settled more securely into the crook of his arm. She was drifting off to sleep, vaguely aware she should finish the sentence.

He stroked her soft hair with his hand as her eyes closed and her breathing slowed. *Which one of us is boring?* he asked himself. She was sound asleep, snuggled against him as trusting as a child. Their conversation would have to wait. He scooped her up and carried her to her bed.

Her eyes flitted open as he lay her down.

"Good night," she sighed.

He lowered his head and kissed her gently.

She responded as he dreamed she would, kissing him back. His arms were around her, he wanted to deepen the kiss, but her body went limp.

He pulled back. She was fast asleep. She must have been exhausted. Of course, she had early mornings and grueling physical days on Desolation Sound. As innocently as a child, she'd lost her battle to stay awake. He kissed her forehead.

"Good night, precious Julie." Never had he found courting a woman so difficult.

He tiptoed from the room and closed the door soundlessly.

The first rays of morning light struck the ivy-covered walls of the grand old hotel. Julie was already up and dressed, poring over her list of things to buy, adding several items of her own, planning her shopping strategy, anxious to begin. It was barely six o'clock, the stores wouldn't be open for hours but she was restless and eager to begin, accustomed to rising with the sun.

Cautiously she opened her bedroom door, planning to take a walk in the hotel's rose garden, careful not to wake her host. But she was stopped in her tracks, halfway across the sitting room by a deep demanding voice.

"Where are you going?"

She hadn't anticipated him up this early, shaved and immaculately dressed in suit and tie. If Greek gods wore business suits, this is how they'd look, and first thing in the morning too.

"I . . . I thought I'd take a walk."

"Without breakfast?"

"I didn't want to wake you."

He crossed the sitting room in three long strides and turned her to face him, his hands warm against her upper arms. "I've been awake for a while." He didn't mention he'd been tossing and turning through the night thinking about this woman, who was trying to sneak out on him before he had a chance to say all the things he'd been planning.

"Will you join me for breakfast, downstairs in the dining room?"

She smiled her acceptance. "I'd love to. Could I walk in the hotel gardens first? And check out the conservatory?"

"By all means." He extended his arm to escort her through the door. "I could do with a breath of fresh air myself this morning."

They toured the hotel grounds, still damp with dew, a tall handsome man, dapper in a dark gray business suit, and a sprightly young woman with an unruly mass of dark curly hair in a delicate pink sweater and flowing skirt. It may only have been a garden oasis in the midst of city streets, but it was how she remained in his mind, natural, honest, and beautifully windswept, surrounded by lush growing plants, nothing artificial about her.

"Are you always this cheerful in the morning?"

"I like mornings, a new start, full of promise, and energy enough to tackle anything."

"Indeed." He knew for a fact that Nicole Ashton never rose before eleven o'clock, and even then, it took her hours to apply makeup and dress. "Shall we go in now? They may agree to serve breakfast in the conservatory; no one else seems to be around. We are the only early-risers in the hotel."

"City life," Julie chuckled. "No chickens to feed, no goat to milk."

"Would you choose it permanently over life on Desolation Sound?"

Julie looked up into his solemn face. Her answer seemed important to him. "That's a tough question. Each has its merits." She paused to consider. "Living in town would have to be my choice. Homesteading is much too difficult for a single person alone."

Andrew nodded. "It's a challenging lifestyle."

They ate in the humid, glassed-in room amidst potted plants, trickling water and lush greenery. As she spread marmalade on her toast, he asked, "Where will you start?"

"The art store, it's closest. Then I'll find a good book store . . . I could spend all day choosing books but your helicopter will never get off the ground if I buy every book that appeals to me."

She likes books too, he added to his list of things he knew about Julie. He smiled at her over his coffee cup. "I see you have your day well planned."

"I'm looking forward to it; I haven't been shopping in three months." She didn't mention the ship chandler's and the toy store also on her list.

"Then you'll need this." He pulled a credit card from his pocket and handed it to her.

"Oh no! I couldn't take that."

"You can and you will. I insist."

Her fingers closed around the piece of plastic. She had her own credit card, bankcard and checkbook with her. She looked into the stern blue eyes studying her, and gulped. He wouldn't take no for an answer. Probably he thought she would bankrupt the Corwins with a wild spending spree.

"Thank you." She smiled up at him guilelessly. She had no intention of using his credit card but he was sweet to offer it. "That's generous of you."

"Use it," he said, as if guessing her intentions.

"Aren't you afraid I'll put you in the poorhouse with a pile of exorbitant purchases?"

"No. You say little about yourself, but I've observed you are scrupulously moral and honest to the core."

She blushed pink to the very roots of her hair at this last statement. Oh, if only he knew. "I . . ."

He found her blush charming, folded her fingers tightly around his credit card and pushed back his chair. He turned up his cuff to look at his watch. "Shall we go? The stores will soon be opening, and I have a meeting to get to."

They parted outside the Tracklin suite—Julie with her shoulder bag, and Andrew with his briefcase. "I'll meet you here at six o'clock. We can have dinner, then fly back to Desolation Sound."

Julie nodded agreement. He looked incredibly dashing, standing there looking down at her with that strange expression. She impulsively stood on tiptoe and kissed him on his astonished lips.

"Good luck with your meeting today."

And then the elevator door swished closed and she was gone before he could say anything or return that kiss the way he wanted to.

Julie set off at a brisk pace toward the art shop on Fort Street. Late summer flowers cascaded in colorful profusion from hanging baskets on every lamppost. Tour buses and guides waited outside The Empress to show off the quaint English heritage of a city more English than England.

She passed souvenir shops and Indian craft displays before turning into the place she wanted. Besides Anna's canvasses and oils, she selected watercolor papers for Daniel, brushes, sketchpads, vibrant neon felt markers for the children, and a coloring book of animals for Simon.

"Will that be cash or charge, ma'am?"

"Charge, please." She handed the girl her credit card, her fingers passing over the card Andrew had given her. She tucked it firmly to the back of her purse. *I must remember to return it.*

"Can you have those delivered to The Empress by five o'clock today?"

"No trouble, ma'am. Room number?"

Julie couldn't recall any room number, not even which floor it was on.

"Address it to the Tracklin suite. That should do it."

"Very good, ma'am. Enjoy your stay in Victoria."

Julie smiled. "Thank you."

She'd forgotten how pleasant it was being amongst people, chatting and passing the time of day. Even strangers looked fascinating to her this morning.

American tourists were beginning to fill the streets, cameras slung around their necks, shopping for Indian carvings, English china and Cuban cigars. Julie slipped past a tour party milling about on the sidewalk and into a bookshop.

Paradise. The new titles near the entrance were deliciously tempting but she stuck to her plan and found the children's section first. The illustrations were wonderful, the stories lively, and if she had enough time, she could settle down in that conveniently placed armchair and skim through every one on display.

It took discipline, but Julie managed to choose five books for each child, ones she was sure they'd enjoy, and among them was that tugboat picture book for Simon. Anna and Daniel weren't neglected either; her arms were loaded with a volume on west coast history, two murder mysteries, an organic foods cookbook, three art books and several of those bestsellers so enticingly displayed beside the cashier's desk. The long wet winter would not be boring on Desolation Sound.

While paying, and arranging for delivery to the hotel, she found her watch in the bottom of her purse. She slipped it on her wrist, a delicate antique face on a slim gold band. Its familiar presence reaffirmed the fact that she was Julie, a chemical engineer, who hadn't noticed time or worn a watch since the day she left Vancouver. Her usual self was surfacing.

Rogers Candy Shop beckoned as she was looking for a jewelry store. The chocolate-dipped candy pieces were large, so she only sampled two, but she made a careful selection for the Corwins, including everyone's favorites. She was enjoying this, like playing Santa Claus. She earned a generous salary, something she'd gladly share with Anna and her family; now was her chance and she loved every minute of it.

The tortoise shell barrettes for Moira were easy to find, and the Swiss army knife for Jake she had engraved with his initials. Her carrier bag was getting heavy with the clothes for Anna and the gloves for Daniel. She'd done a complete circle through the shopping district and wasn't far from the hotel. Her stomach rumbled; she'd missed lunch. She checked her watch—time to drop her recent purchases at the hotel, grab a quick lunch, then make it to the ship chandler's and back by six o'clock.

From the office of the forestry minister, Andrew Tracklin looked across the inner harbor to the grounds of The Empress, thronged with tourists in the afternoon sun, and horse-drawn sightseeing tours competing with red double-decker buses. A delectable pink sweater and long flowing skirt caught his eye. She was in a hurry, cutting a direct path to the hotel, a large carrier bag over her arm. She didn't look out of place away from her wilderness solitude. She didn't dither and gawk about like the foreign tourists swarming the streets. He smiled as she dipped into the hotel—a woman with a purpose.

He turned back to the debate before him, determined to have it finished in good time.

Julie surveyed the mountain of packages on the floor of the Tracklin suite; she'd gotten everything on her list. Could one helicopter hold this much? She was frowning over this dilemma when Andrew walked in.

"Problems?"

He looked wonderful, tall and distinguished, nothing like those pushy tourists in garish, brightly colored summer shorts who'd been elbowing her all day.

"Have I overdone it? Can all this fit in a helicopter?"

"Easily." His eyes were to drown in when he smiled like that. She quickly looked away so he wouldn't see her staring. "Successful shop?"

"Marvelous! I got everything I wanted."

He noticed she was still wearing the same outfit in which she'd left Desolation Sound. Presumably, new clothes weren't among the things she wanted—another fact about Julie to add to his list. And another comparison with Nicole Ashton; that woman never passed a clothing store without buying something.

She reached for her purse and dug out his credit card.

"Thank you." She handed it to him, glowing with the day's activity, happy she'd remembered to give back the card she hadn't used, but not lifting her head to meet his eyes.

"Did you use it?"

She couldn't return the probing look he directed at her. She looked down at her feet and nodded. "It was very kind of you."

Was she shy about accepting money from him? Had he embarrassed her? He didn't want to dampen her spirits. She seemed uncomfortable about something. Damn, but this woman was a mystery.

"Are you ready for dinner? I've made a reservation in the dining room; I, for one, am starving. Talking to politicians gives me an appetite."

That eased the tense moment. Julie was hungry, too, and thoughts of food distracted her from the guilt she felt at not telling him the truth. She had money of her own and didn't use his; he'd find that out at the end of the month when his bill arrived.

They ate a superb meal served on a fine white tablecloth, with gold-embossed china and highly polished silverware. Andrew noticed she wasn't ill at ease in the posh surroundings, she didn't stare about the room in awe, or have difficulty ordering; perhaps she was too excited to realize she wasn't still at a simple scrubbed wooden table in a remote windswept house.

"Tell me what you bought."

"Oh, everything—books, paint supplies, toys, a Swiss army knife and of course, Rogers chocolate. No trip to Victoria could be complete without that!"

"Did you have trouble finding your way around?"

"No. Everyone is so friendly."

Remarkable—she wasn't put off by city congestion and unfamiliar streets. And she's not shy. He thought she'd be overwhelmed, coming from her quiet, uninhabited background. *Maybe it's all an adventure to her, like hiking in the forest or sailing in rough seas.*

"You must be anxious to get all your purchases home."

"Yes." She looked at him with happiness sparkling in her velvet brown eyes, a look he guessed was eagerness to unpack her new possessions. "It's fun to share treasures, isn't it?"

That remark left him speechless. He knew not *all* of those packages were for herself; the art supplies for Anna and the Swiss army knife for Jake. Were *any* of them?

Surely she hadn't spent the day shopping and bought nothing for herself?

He'd pay special attention when these bags and boxes were opened. No woman he knew could resist clothes, shoes, jewelry, perfume—all the expensive things Nicole Ashton spent her days selecting. But then, Julie was unique—he didn't know what to expect from her next.

The hotel staff efficiently bundled all of Julie's packages into a taxi. The generous tip from the gentleman may have helped.

Thankfully, it fit into the helicopter. Julie positively vibrated with happy anticipation. The Corwin home came into view, snug and peaceful, soft evening light bathing it in a peachy glow as the sun cast its setting rays across the water.

"You love it here, don't you?"

"It's beautiful," Julie answered. "But it saddens me to think it could all be destroyed."

"Destroyed?"

"You know, the mountain stripped of trees, the ocean bare of fish, the air smoggy."

"This means a lot to you."

"It does. I hope the destructive practices are stopped before it's too late."

"Is this an attack on Tracklin's logging?"

Julie gave him a serious look. "Yes, Mr. Tracklin. It is."

"Point taken. It *is* possible to manage the forests with minimum impact on the environment."

"It's possible. But is it being done?"

"Touché."

The children were already in their pajamas, preparing to leave early the next morning for their grandparents. They came skipping across the pasture barefoot to hug their aunt

and welcome her, each carrying an armful of her bags and boxes back to the house.

Andrew watched the unwrapping very closely. The children squealed delight at books, toys and felt pens; Anna kissed Julie when she took out the beautiful sweater and matching slacks; unable to wait, Daniel began reading the first page of the book chosen for him.

Amidst hugs and kisses and gasps of pleasure, no empty wrappings accumulated at Julie's feet. There was one paper bag still untouched, though.

Noticing his attentive blue eyes so carefully taking in the scene, Julie picked up the sturdy brown bag and came to sit beside him.

She dazzled him with a radiant smile. "This is for you."

Automatically, he accepted the plain package, startled to be included in the gift giving. His usually adept fingers fumbled removing the box from inside the brown paper bag. He couldn't guess what it contained and it didn't matter. Her generosity touched a place in his heart that had been cynical and doubting until she lit it with her wholesome, kind gesture.

It contained an exclusive nautical hand-held compass, unlike any he'd seen before.

She could see he was taken by surprise and hastened to explain.

"You only have a fixed compass in your cabin. You can take this one with you to the transom. Anna and I found it invaluable in a race, for keeping on course."

Hearing her name, Anna came over to admire it. "She's right. You'll find it priceless."

"I'm sure I will. Thank you." His voice almost failed him, it was not the strong, confident sound associated with Andrew Tracklin. It was quiet, hesitant, struggling with some deep emotion.

She was smiling at him with that honest, open, lovable expression of hers. How do you thank a woman properly

in front of a crowd of people? He wanted to kiss her, the way she was looking up at him. It was the perfect gift and he felt helpless to express the depth of his appreciation. Merely thanking her was so inadequate.

It was then he noticed the splendid watch on her wrist. A shaft of pleasure pierced him. She *had* used his credit card to buy something for herself. He couldn't account for the flush of heat this filled him with. He felt intoxicated, yet he hadn't been drinking.

Anna, still admiring the ship's compass, looked to where his eyes were focused.

"Julie, are you still wearing Granny's watch? I can't believe it still works after all this time!"

His brief moment of sunshine was darkened by clouds, the heat replaced by an icy chill.

Unaware of the turmoil behind those masculine blue eyes, Anna straightened and directed her attention to her children. "Off to bed with you three. We have to make an early start in the morning."

That was also the cue for Andrew Tracklin to make his departure. He could take a hint, even kindly given as Anna's had been. He didn't want to disrupt the smooth running of this lovely family.

He wished each of the Corwins good night, returned his amazing gift to its bag, and carried it with him as he walked to the door. He reached out to Julie with his other hand. He hadn't wished her good night and understanding his wordless message, she took his hand and accompanied him through the pasture to his helicopter.

Feeling tongue-tied and a little breathless, her voice was low. He had to bend his head close to hear. "Thank you for taking me to Victoria. I had a wonderful time, like a fairy tale—no chores, no cooking, no worries . . ."

"Do you have worries, Julie?"

His concern was gentle and coaxing. Now was the time to tell him . . . to confess her real identity.

Her brown eyes stared up at him and the words were strangled in her throat. "I . . . I didn't use your credit card . . ."

He hugged her against his chest, his tangy cologne making her giddy. Thinking she was explaining she hadn't bought his gift with his own money, he gave it no more thought.

She still wore that sweater that felt like crushed rose petals under his fingertips. He stroked her back and tilted her head so he could look into her face.

"Thank you . . . for the compass, which I will treasure . . . and for thinking of me on such a busy day." He had more to say, questions to ask, plans to make . . . but she looked so delectable.

He lowered his head and kissed her, the long leisurely kiss of a man besotted. He kissed away all the explanations she was planning to make, and all the reasons he had for a relationship with this woman being impossible . . . and she kissed him back.

They pulled back, both breathless, hearts pounding.

"Good night," he whispered, not trusting himself to touch her again. "I enjoyed our trip to Victoria too."

He quickly slipped behind the controls and gestured her to move clear of the blades.

She listened to the noisy clatter fade into the distance.

I didn't tell him.

Chapter Eight

"So . . . how did he react?"

"React to what?"

The two sisters were packing a cooler chest with food for the boat trip to Parksville.

"React to you being a city girl with a career."

Julie concentrated her full attention on pouring hot coffee into two thermoses.

"Julie! You didn't tell him, did you?"

"Well . . . he made this comment about me being so honest and moral . . . what could I do . . . blurt out that it's all a lie?" She screwed the tops on the thermoses and placed them on the table. Her troubled brown eyes kept Anna from lecturing.

Remorse made Julie's voice quaver. "Anna, I tried."

"Keeping secrets doesn't make for a lasting relationship."

"Anna, I don't think we're talking about a lasting relationship here. Let him keep his dream. He thinks he met a wisp of his imagination—a perfect nymph from the woods, untouched by civilization, as carefree as the birds in the trees." Julie fluttered her arms in the air, mimicking the flight of birds.

126

"I'm not so sure. I think you're wrong. The man *is* interested."

Julie looked sad. "It's like meeting someone at summer camp. You vow to be friends for life, but once back in your own homes, you send a letter or two . . . and then the excitement fizzles out . . . and all is forgotten."

Anna took one last look around her kitchen to be sure they hadn't missed anything important, then picked up the thermoses to carry to the boat while Julie struggled with the cooler chest.

"It's not the end. The way he looks at you, it's a wonder the ground doesn't catch fire beneath your feet."

"You have such an imagination! When I return to Vancouver, I'll no longer be the untamed spirit of Desolation Sound, and Andrew Tracklin wouldn't recognize me if he saw me." She tried to sound cheerful, but the wobble in her voice gave her away.

They were on the dock beside the Corwin boat, the children fastened into their life jackets, hopping about on deck, eager to cast off. Daniel took the cooler from Julie and set it aboard.

"Are you okay with this, Julie? There's plenty of wood chopped, the chickens are penned, everything is tied down, and the house is secure."

"Don't worry, Daniel. I'll be fine."

Anna hugged Julie and kissed her. She didn't have to put in words what was so evident on her face. She loved her sister, was grateful for all she'd done, and would miss her terribly when they parted after this trip. She thought she was making a mistake, not telling Andrew Tracklin about her life in the city. But Julie's mind was made up and nothing Anna could say would change it. The outcome would rest in the hands of fate.

Julie stood alone on the dock and cast the mooring line aboard.

"One thing!" Daniel called out. "Latch the shutters on the tool shed if the wind picks up! I've left them open!"

Julie smiled and waved as the gap between boat and dock widened. "Don't worry, I'll take care of things! Have fun!"

She watched from the dock until the Corwins' boat was merely a speck in the distance, then turned and walked back to the house, the morning dew burning off in steamy clouds as the sun touched the damp grass. The stillness and lonely silence settled around her. She'd miss this place.

Julie threw herself into a frenzy of activity; her last week on Desolation Sound would be productive. She did a thorough house cleaning, something Anna had been unable to do since her broken arm and leg. The windows sparkled, the waxed floor shone, every pot glistened and the wood stove was scoured so thoroughly it looked new, every trace of ash and soot banished. Julie hung the last of the clean starched curtains she had ironed; the cumbersome flat iron took forever to heat on the stove, but the result was worth it. This house looked like a page out of *Better Homes and Gardens.* Anna would be thrilled.

No sound of voices or scuffle of feet disturbed her household chores. Julie attacked the pile of mending Anna had pushed to the back of a closet. As she sewed on buttons, patched jeans, and let down cuffs, she reflected in the empty silence.

"It's not the end," Anna had said. But if felt like the end to Julie. Her ordinary life bore no resemblance to the way Andrew had seen her here. This was Anna's life, dedicated to husband and family, at peace in solitude and isolation. Julie enjoyed the city lights and fast-paced life in town, with all its distractions and entertainments. The woman Andrew saw here was merely a temporary visitor. It was an illusion, to vanish as quickly as dew on the grass when the sun hit it. She had a life to return to.

Andrew Tracklin is a very attractive man; he must have

his choice of hundreds of women. Too bad I can't be as uncomplicated as he thinks I am. This is just a small part of who I am. I wasn't trying to deceive him. It was essential to fill the role of homesteading wife while Anna needed help, but sadly, that need has passed and Julie was no longer necessary. Her time on Desolation Sound was coming to an end.

She put the mended clothing in the appropriate drawers and went outside to the vegetable garden. A thorough weeding and hoeing would leave it ready for next spring's planting. The light faded before she was finished. She closed the chickens in their roost and went inside to eat a solitary dinner, then fall into an exhausted sleep.

When the rooster crowed next morning, Julie had bread already rising and cookies about to go into the oven. The Corwins would be back tomorrow morning and she wanted everything to be perfect.

As she gathered late summer vegetables, a stiff breeze chilled her bare legs. She stared out across the water, gray and choppy beneath a cloudy sky. The wind was picking up.

By the time her vegetable soup was simmering on top of the stove, she could hear the shutters banging against the tool shed. She hurried out and latched them as Daniel had instructed. White caps topped the waves now, and the fluffy clouds were dark and heavy with rain. A storm was brewing.

Julie carried wood to fill the box beside the stove, closed all the windows, and filled the water reservoir. Her bread filled the kitchen with a fragrant, yeasty aroma as she pulled the loaves from the oven. All was in readiness to welcome the Corwins home. Fresh flowers were on the table, curried chicken was cooked, ready to be reheated, and Julie was rolling out pastry for an apple pie.

By the time the cinnamon and apple pie spices wafted through the house, the sky had darkened and Julie needed to light a lamp. The roar of wind made an eerie sound as it swept across the sea and slammed into the west side of the Corwin house. Julie shivered.

Dusk was settling over Desolation Sound. The sun had slipped below the horizon and the last glimmers of faint light pierced the dense blanket of gray cloud hunched over the sea. The clouds were thickening, getting darker, and the sea reflected their ominous color, cold and black.

The chill of early September made Julie's fingers numb and stiff as she latched the chicken coop, making sure the hens were on their roosts, safe for the night. The first splat of rain stung against her face as she scurried across the yard.

The wind was strong. Her head was down and she was intent on getting back to the house, when a bright flash caught the corner of her eye. Julie stopped and turned toward the sea, lifting her arm to shelter her eyes from the wind and rain, straining to see. It was cold.

The sky was dark, with only the sound of waves splashing on the rocky shore and wind whipping through the bushes at the edge of the garden. Julie thought she'd imagined that light and was turning to get back to the warmth of the wood stove and cozy kitchen, when she saw it again, this time much brighter, shooting straight up into the sky— a red flare, someone in distress.

She strained to see in the fading glow from the flare. Someone was out on the water, perhaps a boat in trouble, out of fuel, on the rocks. Miles from anywhere, who but Julie could see that flare? Daniel and Anna were in Parksville with the children; Julie was alone, and it was up to her to do something. She knew what it was like to be in danger at sea; no one could last long in such cold water.

She did the only thing possible—she ran down the dock, untied the small rowboat, then started rowing toward the spot the flare had originated. The wind had stirred up considerable waves but Julie was strong. She worked the oars confidently. When she was near where she thought the flare was set off, she looked about, taking her bearings. All was dark, with wind swishing above her and waves splashing against the side of the boat.

She called out, "Hello! Can you hear me?"

She held her breath and listened, willing a voice to call in answer.

"Hello! Anyone out here?"

This time, there was a faint reply. Julie rowed in the direction of the voice. It couldn't be far. The wind was loud in her ears, it was a miracle she heard it at all.

"Here," a weak voice gasped, only yards in front of Julie.

Two heads bobbed in the water, orange life jackets secured around their chests, and no sign of a boat or how they'd gotten here.

Julie reached the couple—a man and woman, both middle-aged and immobilized with cold and shock, but both conscious, eyes haunted and faces strained.

"Are you hurt?"

No answer. Two pairs of eyes stared at her from what they were certain was their watery grave.

She anchored the oars and reached down to grasp the woman's life jacket and asked again, "Are you injured? Can you move?"

The man sputtered, then coughed. "My shoulder . . . it hurts. My wife . . . she can't swim. Rocks . . . hole in the hull."

His lips were chattering. Julie could see the cold was beginning to take its toll. She hadn't long before hypothermia set in.

"If you can tread water a little while longer, I can pull your wife into the boat." Her voice sounded cheerful and confident, a great act because she felt neither. She took a lifesaver's hold on the speechless woman and heaved upward. Thankfully she was able to help and landed in the bottom of the boat like a beached whale, dripping wet and gasping for breath.

Julie kept her voice calm and instructed the man to come alongside the rowboat. She grabbed hold of his life jacket, careful to spare his hurt shoulder, and assisted him into the tiny boat. His wife had managed to pull herself upright and sat aft as her husband huddled at the bow. Slowly they set off for the Corwins' dock, Julie using all her strength to row the heavy load.

She could glimpse the lantern she had set in the kitchen window. She used it as a beacon to aim for, a guide to keep her on course. She thought of nothing else, automatically breathing, and pulling the oars, only determination kept her moving the little boat through the water. No longer chilly, she was too numb and exhausted to even feel the cold.

She had no idea how long she'd been rowing through the choppy sea, she ached all over, her leaden arms kept moving, and she snatched gasps of air with each stroke.

Her mind was wandering; she heard a voice calling to her, a comforting voice.

"You're almost to the dock—only a few more yards."

Julie blinked and stared without seeing. She couldn't let this hallucination stop her progress. The boat thumped into the dock's pilings.

"Let go, Julie," the deep voice vibrated in her ear. "I'll take over now."

Those were the words she wanted to hear. Was her mind playing tricks on her?

The elderly man at the bow passed the mooring line to Andrew's outstretched hand.

The boat was secured and the drenched couple assisted onto the dock, shivering, unsteady on their rubbery legs, in shock, but alive and breathing.

Then Andrew scooped Julie out of the boat onto the windswept dock. She clung to him as he held her against his chest.

She felt warmed through by his voice murmuring, "Hold on, love. You're all safe now."

Somehow she was transported to a spot in front of the wood stove, the firebox was filled, and heat emanated in glorious waves. Water droplets sizzled on the stove's surface as Julie leaned over; someone was rubbing life back into her aching arms and wringing out her tangled mass of sopping hair. She closed her eyes then, and let the dream take over.

A gust of wind pushed through the door as Andrew hauled the two boaters into the kitchen. His eyes went to Julie, motionless beside the stove. Her color was back to normal; he let out a sigh of relief. The elderly couple was cold and wet but out of danger. He settled them in front of the hot stove with towels and blankets.

Then he reached for Julie, murmuring her name. She opened her eyes and he told her the two boaters were safe, and turned her so she could see them.

His message registered in her muddled brain. As soon as her eyes settled on the couple sitting by the fire, her bones turned to mush and she slumped into a heap right there on the floor beside the stove.

It was a wonderful dream.

She was drifting in a sunny paradise, something heated and soft caressing her face. It was blissfully warm. Julie opened her eyes, drowsy and unfocused. She was delirious; everything had an unreal quality. She was stretched on a sofa, bundled in a quilt, dry and warm and dreamy—no wind or rain or water. She knew she must be imagining it but she didn't want to wake up.

A warm mug was pressed into her hands.

"Drink this."

The voice was familiar—it was a lovely voice—and so were the fathomless blue eyes. She didn't think her wrinkled fingers or her rubbery arms could support the mug but the vision pressed it to her lips.

"Sip. That's an order." The voice was husky and deep; she was too weak to argue.

Obediently, she sipped—then choked and coughed. Her face flushed as the drink trickled down her throat and spread heat into every nerve ending numbed by cold. It tasted vile.

Her wide eyes stared accusingly at the man holding the cup. His smile warmed her.

"Hot rum," he said. "Revives even drowned men."

Heat burned through her, her mind cleared slightly, and Julie looked around, finally taking in her surroundings. She was back in the Corwins' kitchen. An assortment of unfamiliar clothing hung from the drying rack above the wood stove. It was all rather blurry.

Andrew Tracklin knelt beside her, his damp hair curling along the collar of that lovely red sweater she'd laundered and left waiting to return to him. The expression on his face wasn't one she'd seen before—neither arrogant nor teasing, just clear blue eyes swallowing her up as if she were water in a dry parched desert.

"Feeling better?"

She nodded, shyly realizing she had nothing on under the quilt.

He gestured to the two people, wrapped in blankets, sitting on chairs either side of the blazing wood stove. "Mr. and Mrs. Ralston owe you their lives."

She remembered the flare and rowing out to rescue them, but she had questions. He read her thoughts.

"Their wooden boat was holed on the rocks and sank in minutes. They only had time to send a distress call, then set off two flares."

A shaky voice from beside the fire continued the story. "We didn't think there was any chance of being seen, what with the wind picking up like it was, no one was out on the water." He patted his wife's hand. "May isn't a swimmer . . . we couldn't have lasted long." His soulful eyes zeroed in on Julie. "You saved our lives. We can't thank you enough."

His wife wiped her eyes with the corner of the blanket. "Thank you," she whispered. "I was so frightened." Her husband took her hand in his.

"Now, May, none of that. You set off those flares and helped save us both."

She looked gratefully at her husband, weary and relieved. She knew his shoulder was in pain but still he thought of her safety first.

Brief snatches were playing back in Julie's mind. It seemed so far away, like images from a movie. She was so tired.

Julie's voice was hoarse. "I had help." She stared at Andrew, wondering how he fit in. How had he appeared at the moment he was needed? Or had she just imagined it?

He answered before she had a chance to ask. "I heard the SOS in the helicopter. I had delivered engine parts to the logging camp and was near enough to help."

He watched Julie struggling to sit up. She didn't look like she had the strength left to breathe let alone sit upright. He put his arm around her waist to support her. Her legs slid off the sofa and she began to wiggle her bare toes, bringing back feeling, unaware of the enticing length of bare leg exposed.

He drew a deep breath. She didn't know what she was doing to him. "Why are you alone here?"

Julie's muddled thoughts came out in a jumble. "Daniel's parents . . . the children . . . visit." She looked at him as though it all made perfect sense.

"When will they be back?"

His soft voice made her smile. "Tomorrow."

He hoped she would understand. He didn't want to leave her like this. His worried face was close to her ear as he gently lifted her legs back onto the sofa. "Mr. Ralston needs a doctor." He stopped and studied her sweet face. "I must fly them to hospital now."

He couldn't keep the concern out of his voice. "Will you be all right here?"

Julie was in a dreamy state, at the edge of much-needed sleep, hallucinating. A radiant smile filled her drawn face. "That would be nice."

"Don't move, love. You need to keep warm and sleep."

"Sleep," she repeated.

She wasn't making much sense, she'd pushed herself to the limit; he was reluctant to leave her.

He looked across at the couple by the fire. They were dry and warm but Mr. Ralston was squirming in his chair, obviously in pain. The weight of his arm was supported in a sling, but the lines of pain on his face called out for medical attention. The sooner he got to a hospital, the better.

Julie's head was back against a pillow, she was still smiling and mumbling, off in a world of her own, her heavy eyelids were impossible to keep open any longer.

Andrew tucked a blanket snugly around her, lowered his head and kissed her lips, cutting off her mumbled stream of disconnected words.

"Sleep now, sweetheart. We'll talk tomorrow."

She was sound asleep before he had banked the fire, straightened the kitchen, and ushered the grateful couple across the pasture to his helicopter. The wind had eased; rain washed Desolation Sound in a soft gray mist as the helicopter lifted and headed to Powell River.

For once, Julie didn't hear the clatter of its blades. But she was dreaming of its pilot, there when she needed him. She loved him.

The sun was high in the sky when Geraldine's bleating woke Julie from a deep sleep. She rubbed her eyes . . . the rum . . . the faint taste on her lips raised questions. She scanned the empty room. Her week of intense housecleaning showed—the waxed floor shone, freshly washed curtains hung at the windows . . . but two chairs were out of place . . . beside the stove . . . her rumpled jeans and sweater were on the drying rack above the stove, her underwear too. She looked down at the quilt and blanket covering her; she could feel the scratchiness of the wool against her bare skin. She lifted the blanket and checked . . . she was completely naked, and sleeping on the sofa.

Slowly, glimpses of the past night's events played out in her mind.

It wasn't entirely clear. It probably was a dream. But . . . no . . . there had been a flare . . . and two people in the water. She shook the sleep out of her foggy brain. Then she looked around the sunny kitchen for clues.

Well, those two people weren't here now. They must be safe and on their way.

That explanation didn't seem quite right . . . some pieces were missing, but she couldn't worry about that now. The goat's bleating was insistent. Who knows what damage Geraldine might do if she wasn't tended?

Julie scrambled to her feet, dressed quickly and went to milk the distressed animal.

By the time the day's chores were done—the chickens were set free to scratch and peck about the yard, the wood box filled and water carried up from the well—Julie had convinced herself she'd been imagining things. She'd been alone too long, a sign that it was time to return to Vancouver.

It was early afternoon when a familiar horn sounded from the water. Julie raced to the dock to catch the mooring line Jake tossed her.

"Welcome home."

"Anything exciting happen while we were gone?"

"You wouldn't believe!" She said it with such emphasis, the whole group burst out laughing. They all thought nothing exciting ever happened on Desolation Sound.

The chattering group carried supplies up to the house.

"Still determined to leave today?"

"Yes." Julie nodded. "It's time I go home."

Anna's eyes clouded over. Julie noticed and softened the blow. "I'm needed at work. One of the other engineers has holidays next week."

After three months together, this leave-taking was difficult. *Make it fast,* Julie reasoned. Amidst the hubbub of returning from holiday, she wouldn't be missed right away. Her things packed, precious little clothing was left; her bag was light, unlike her heart.

There were floods of tears as she hugged and kissed her niece and nephews, then her sister. They all knew this day of parting was coming but now that it was here, no one wanted to believe it.

"We couldn't have made it without you," Anna cried. "I know you have to go back . . . but I'll miss you." She hugged her sister close.

Julie cried too. She told herself she should be happy— Anna was glowing with health and walked with barely a limp. The tears wouldn't stop. She took a deep breath, grasped her bag, and stepped aboard Daniel's boat, forcing a brave smile on her face for the benefit of her sister and the children.

Daniel pulled away from the dock and Julie waved until the four figures on the shore were no longer visible.

In his quiet, sensible voice, Daniel congratulated her. "You did a good job . . . for a city girl."

The tension melted away as she laughed at the rare compliment from her brother-in-law. Then the tears began again.

Discreetly, Daniel busied himself skippering the boat. The sky was clear, there was no wind, and the sea was as calm as the water in a bathtub, but he gave the impression of being fully occupied guiding the small craft to meet the ferry to take Julie back to her life in Vancouver.

She mopped her face and took long deep gulps of fresh salt air. She wasn't usually weepy. It must be the sadness of leaving her sister and family. She felt so weary.

A niggling feeling of some task unfinished troubled her, even as the ferry slip came into view. It was all such a rush. She hated prolonged good-byes.

Daniel carried her one small bag and a bundle of canvasses for the gallery, to the ticket booth, gave her a giant bear hug and kissed her soundly. "You saved our skins. Thank you isn't enough, but it comes from the heart. Thank you, Julie."

Holding back tears, she kissed him, then turned and sprinted onto the ferry as its last whistle sounded and it prepared to cast off.

The turbulent wake frothed up by the propellers was nothing compared to the turbulence swirling inside Julie's head. She wanted to return to her apartment, her work, her life in the city.

And she wanted to be the simple, uncomplicated wood nymph Andrew thought she was; wind in her hair, breeze at her back, and nothing more demanding than picking berries or milking goats to challenge her.

But there was more to her than that—she loved her sister and her family and she also loved her work, fine clothes, comfortable furnishings, evenings at the theater, classical music . . . he had never seen that side of her. How would he feel about it? She ached at her cowardice in not telling him.

She was leaving more than Desolation Sound. She was leaving that carefree part of her, in tattered shorts and fly-away hair, behind as well.

She should feel happy returning to her familiar life—but her tears wouldn't stop; she felt torn in two.

Chapter Nine

Andrew swerved his racy car along Beach Road past the glass and concrete forest of high-rise apartments overlooking English Bay. Dark clouds were reflected in the slate-gray sea, cold and choppy, and a damp chill fanned his face through the open car window—typical rainy Vancouver weather.

Past windshield wipers barely able to keep up with the downpour, he scanned the address numbers, at the same time searching for a parking spot somewhere amidst the expensive cars lining the street.

How could Julie afford living in the west end? Prices here were as sky-high as the buildings. She'd been vague about the work she did.

The more he thought about it, she told him nothing about her work. Perhaps she was ashamed; perhaps she keeps house for some wealthy tenant in this posh neighborhood.

Odd, she never mentioned surroundings like this. But then, to be fair, he never gave her the chance. It was the last place he expected to find an unspoiled woman who flourished in the outdoors and simple life.

Spotting the address Anna gave him, he turned sharply

onto the paved entranceway manned by a uniformed doorman.

"May I help you, sir?"

Andrew stalled. He couldn't just ask for Julie. He realized now he didn't know her last name. But Anna had
included an apartment number.

"I wish to see a young lady in Apartment 912."

The doorman gave him a frosty look. "I'm sorry, sir. The
young lady is not in."

"Can I wait in the lobby until she returns?"

"I'm sorry, sir. No admittance uninvited," he said with
such disdain, Andrew withered under his accusing glare.

"Do you know when she'll be back?"

"I'm not at liberty to reveal that, sir."

Frustrated, Andrew's fingers tightened on the steering
wheel, and he cursed under his breath. He took a business
card from his inside pocket. He also looked at the address
Anna had written for him.

It said BEACH ROAD, but it didn't say VANCOUVER. Every
town along the B.C. coast from Washington State to Alaska
has a street named BEACH ROAD or a MARINE DRIVE.

He looked back at the luxurious building. The modest,
simple-living Julie he knew wasn't likely to live here in
this extravagant, modern building. It was all wrong. Or was
it?

Anna assumed he knew which town. He jumped to the
wrong conclusion. How could he have thought she was a
part of this noisy, crowded, polluted, city scene?

He growled a curse at the card still in his hand.

"Do you wish to leave your card, sir?"

"No . . . no. I've gotten the wrong address."

"Very good, sir. Good day."

He crushed the card in his hand, then, on squealing tires,
pulled back into traffic heading south for the airport.

At Desolation Sound, Julie had left no message for him,

no good-bye, no hope that they'd meet again. She just vanished, as though she had never been, like a dream that fades into the subconscious upon waking. And now he was on his way to Japan with a trade commission, no way to contact the Corwins, no way to find Julie.

Damn! He'd find her. She was not a dream; she was a flesh and blood woman like none he'd encountered before. *I'll find her no matter what secret she's hiding.*

As he idled at the red light, the thought occurred to him that perhaps she didn't want to be found. She wasn't married but that didn't say she wasn't involved with someone.

She made no promises. She did nothing to encourage him. She left no trace.

She was hiding something.

The driver behind him leaned on his horn. The light was green. Andrew accelerated across the intersection.

She can't do this to me. Just when I realize how much she means to me, she's gone. I can't pretend she never existed; she's there in every breath I take.

I'll find her. I must.

The colorful, glossy travel brochures were still on the coffee table exactly as Julie left them three months ago. The cleaning lady had been in; the carpets were vacuumed, no film of dust marred the polished wood surfaces. All was as it had been.

Except Julie.

After one look in the well-lit bathroom mirror, she reached for the telephone to make a hairdresser appointment. Her tangle of curly hair reached past her shoulders, knotted, impossible to pass even a brush through. Tying it back with a ribbon might be acceptable by candlelight on Desolation Sound but it wouldn't pass muster under unforgiving electric lights at Northern Chemicals.

Her tan was darker than she realized; she could've taken that Hawaiian vacation as planned. From the outside, she looked like she'd enjoyed a pampered holiday, laying on the white sands, splashing in the surf, eating tropical fruit . . .

She pursed her lips and stared blankly at the view of English Bay through her picture window. She'd eaten tropical fruit a handsome blue-eyed man brought as a gift. It wasn't the standard candy and flowers. He put thought into it. It was personal, exactly right. He was very good at doing and saying what was exactly right.

She would probably never see him again and that hurt more than she imagined it ever would.

Her time on Desolation Sound was like a chapter in a storybook, a lovely story but all pretend. Now the page was turned. Back to reality. No happy ending.

She changed into tailored slacks and sandals and searched out her car keys—first the bank machine, then the grocery store. Her cupboards were bare; life had to go on. She wished she could talk it out with Anna, but she was far away. *You're on your own, girl, you can handle this. Take one step at a time. Isn't that what Grandfather said?* She took a deep breath, unfastened her seat belt and made that first step across the paved parking lot, back into her previously satisfying life—great apartment, successful career, no financial worries and an active social life.

Opportunities lost were best forgotten; regrets would only reduce her to tears.

The painful, empty gap where her heart had been wasn't visible to anyone watching the confident, well-dressed woman walking to the bank machine.

The luxuries missed on Desolation Sound now filled her grocery cart—bagels, cream cheese, ice cream, fresh orange juice and bananas.

She'd trade all of them for another chance with Andrew Tracklin.

She'd brought the hurt on herself, she hadn't been truthful; she couldn't expect him to trust her.

As she packed her groceries into the trunk of her car, she wished he didn't occupy her every waking moment. She couldn't escape him even when she was asleep. The hurt would lessen, she promised herself. She would forget.

"How long has it been since you last had your hair cut?"

"Four . . . five months."

"Look at this! There's more hair on the floor than on most people's heads."

Julie watched the dark mass of curls being swept up. Her short hair was stylishly sleek, shaped to flatter her tanned face.

"A change in hairstyle; a change in life. That's how the saying goes." The hairdresser held up a mirror for Julie to see the back of her cropped head. "What do you think?"

It was definitely a change. Short and sassy, the hairdresser called it.

"I bet you've lost five pounds, removing that much hair."

Julie laughed. "It feels lighter."

She tipped the hairdresser, inhaling the fragrance of shampoo, hair spray, curling lotions, and hearing the buzz of hair dryers and the chatter of women. She was back in familiar territory. The Julie of Desolation Sound would soon be only a memory.

A brush of fresh air whispered against the back of her neck as she unlocked her car. She shrugged her shoulders as tiny fragments of hair prickled down her collar.

Daniel's and Anna's paintings were on the back seat of her car, waiting to be delivered to the gallery. She hadn't opened the bundle Daniel put on the ferry with her; it was still in the same brown paper wrapping.

"These are splendid." The gallery owner was setting a series of Daniel's watercolors and Anna's oil paintings against the white wall of his studio.

"Aah . . . this one will fetch a fine price. Marvelous work

. . . captures a feeling of melancholy . . . sadness untouched by the beautiful setting. I love it! I'll feature it in the display window . . . priceless."

He held the oil painting at arm's length and sang its praises. "The light is perfect . . . and that face . . ." He turned to look at Julie. "It's you, isn't it, Miss? The hair is longer but I recognize the haunting face, the . . . er . . . fine figure."

Julie hadn't seen the picture he was gushing over. She stood beside the gallery owner and stared.

Anna had captured her exact expression, longing for something she couldn't have, regretting the words unspoken, the truth untold. She stood at the end of the Corwins' dock, gazing out to sea, waiting for something or someone. But the scene was silent and still, nothing moving, even the clouds were frozen in place. Whatever she was waiting for wasn't coming.

An aching sadness drew the viewer's eyes to the face of the lone woman.

"There's a story behind this portrait." He put his hand over his heart. "Gets you right here, doesn't it?"

Julie nodded and looked away. It hurt to be reminded.

She filled out the appropriate forms allowing the gallery to sell the paintings and made a hasty exit. She didn't want reminders of Desolation Sound that stirred up so much pain.

That chapter was ended. She turned the page. The opportunity was missed. She'd been playing a role, now the curtain had dropped, the play was over and she was back to her everyday life. The yearning, aching sadness was behind her.

Only it wasn't.

"Looking good, Marantse! Were you on some wilderness fitness program? You look lean, ready to climb Mt. Everest."

"I'm ready, Gordon. Join me?"

The portly engineer laughed. "I can barely make it up three flights of stairs." He watched her noting pressure gauge readings. "Good to have you back."

Martin, the project manager, brought her up to date on the latest alterations to the chemical reaction. "We've missed you, Julie. No one to tease."

"I never thought I'd say this but I missed being here."

Martin patted her on the back like a proud father. "Your sister okay?"

"Fine. She has a bit of a limp but that'll go away with exercise."

"There have been several calls from Tracklin's wanting to get in touch with you. It seems they were considering using fenitrothion. That's dangerous stuff. Check at the office; they want to arrange a meeting with you."

"I'll do that."

Martin couldn't put his finger on what had changed about Julie. But something had. That feisty challenge was gone from her eyes. She'd softened. She was slimmer, stronger, and rested, but a world-weary huskiness crept into her voice at times, unlike the cheerful, bubbly Julie he was used to.

"We've put you on afternoon shift, starting next week. Can you handle that?"

"Sure."

"No more 'up with the chickens' for you, eh?"

"No more chickens, Martin. Condos in the west end don't encourage livestock."

He laughed. "Welcome back."

She walked to the computer terminal to enter the readings. Martin stopped at the door before leaving the lab. "Remember, I'm here if you want to talk."

Julie appreciated his fatherly concern. Her eyes filled with tears.

"Thanks, Martin. I'll remember that."

* * *

Did the inquiries from Tracklin's mean Andrew was trying to contact her? She was giddy with hope as she phoned the number. She was put through to an executive secretary who connected her to a member of the board of directors.

"Dr. Marantse, thank you for returning my call. We were impressed by the report you sent concerning spraying on Desolation Sound. Would it be possible for you to make a presentation before the entire board to expand upon your objections? We feel the need to get an educated scientific opinion.

"Yes, I'd be pleased to speak to your directors." Julie kept her voice business-like but she was cheering inside. "Would next Wednesday morning be suitable?"

"I'll put you through to my secretary to make final arrangements. I look forward to meeting you and hearing your presentation."

No mention was made of Andrew Tracklin; she wasn't put through to his personal secretary. Julie was disappointed but there was still a glimmer of hope. She looked forward to Wednesday.

The days passed quickly. Julie worked overtime filling in for others taking vacations. She worked her last afternoon shift, returning home past midnight, let in by the night security guard as the doorman was off duty. She hadn't had a chance to chat with Larkin since her return from Desolation Sound. His uniformed presence at the door seemed a bit much, but it was a security measure the other condo owners insisted on. She wondered how Larkin's family was doing; he had a daughter going to university.

She'd have time to catch up on gossip now that she was back on day shift.

Gradually she resumed her life as a young urban professional. But she failed to harness the thrill of discovery, the excitement her job had previously held. Day by day, the work was uneventful. She was a trained engineer but her skills were being wasted. The chemical plant had no emergencies any more, no malfunctions; everything ran smoothly. She'd done her job too well.

Anyone could read gauges and adjust dials; her expertise wasn't needed here. The job she'd done, setting up the chemical process, was finished. It ran efficiently, no more delicate tuning required.

Julie itched for some new problem to solve, some untried theory to set in motion. Quite simply, she was bored. She never had to deal with such feelings before. Chemistry had kindled a spark of excitement for as long as she remembered. Perhaps she was in a rut.

She joined an exercise class at the gym and accepted invitations to crew in sailing races. The frantic activity didn't leave her time to brood . . . but it didn't rekindle the spark, either.

After a vigorous day of sailing trials, Julie dropped her pack in the middle of her bedroom carpet and checked the messages on her answering machine.

"Hi Julie. Martin here. I was hoping you'd be back by now. I have tickets to the symphony tonight and Ruth is in bed with a dreadful cold. She suggested I take you instead; she doesn't want me moping around the house all evening knowing I'd rather be at the symphony. If you're in before seven o'clock, give me a call."

She checked her watch—5:30. That gave her time to eat a quick meal, change, and meet Martin in time for the opening. She phoned the florist and sent flowers to Ruth, then made arrangements with Martin, dashed about unpacking, then dressing for a formal evening out.

A wolf whistle greeted her in the lobby of her building.

"You look gorgeous. If I weren't old enough to be your father, I'd be smitten."

"You look rather splendid yourself. Evening dress suits you. How's Ruth?"

"Snuffling. She says thanks for the flowers."

"Least I could do, stealing her husband for the evening."

The doorman stepped forward but Martin smoothly tucked her into his car and she only had time to buckle up before the Mercedes pulled away, heading toward the Orpheum Theater.

The concert opened with Handel, and Julie reveled in the peaceful swell of music and the undemanding company of her friend and coworker.

At intermission, they sipped Perrier and chatted about future prospects at Northern Chemicals; a distinguished gray-haired man in evening dress and a lovely dark-haired young woman in a blue designer gown that emphasized her delightful curves, yet gave the impression of being modest.

They didn't go unnoticed by the tall, fair-haired man who was also elegantly dressed, on the other side of the lobby. The woman's back was to him but she caught his attention. From this distance it was impossible, but he swore he heard a hint of Julie's voice, soft and clear and as natural as waves lapping the shore.

That well-dressed woman was too comfortable in these sophisticated surroundings to be the wild breath of fresh air he remembered, yet the curve of her hips and the graceful way she moved made him think of Julie.

He shook his head, then turned to his companion.

Those trips to Desolation Sound were haunting him. Had he imagined the pure joy and simple honesty of that elusive woman? Now he was hearing her voice and believing he saw her in a crowded lobby.

His trip to Japan had given him time to reflect on Julie's unique qualities. He missed his chance. She slipped through his fingers. She was gone without a trace. The shy forest flower, more beautiful because of its rarity, had captured his heart unlike all these hothouse plants—garish, pampered, and mass-produced.

A secret wish wouldn't go away. If she wanted, she

could contact him. Tracklin's offices were listed in the phone book. Dr. Marantse had visited Tracklin's board of directors while he was in Japan and given irrefutable evidence to shoot down David's plans to spray the forests of Desolation Sound. If that chemical engineer could find Tracklin's, so could Julie.

He glanced across the room to get one more look at the woman who couldn't be Julie but captured his attention. She was gone—returned to her seat, intermission over.

The florist's business card atop his morning mail was one of Mrs. Wyatt's subtle hints to "put things right." Andrew ripped it to shreds with a vengeance and watched the tiny bits scatter into his wastepaper basket.

Put things right! Ha!

Mrs. Wyatt ignored the nasty scowl her employer gave as she sat down to take dictation. Mr. Tracklin was in a vicious temper this week, barking orders, slamming doors, and snapping at anyone who dared to telephone.

It wasn't business problems. The quarterly report showed sizable profits. She watched her boss drumming his fingers on his desk as he dictated letters in rapid-fire succession.

A proud man, Mr. Tracklin wouldn't take kindly to rejection by a woman, a totally new experience. *He's too handsome and charming by far. Do him good, a taste of humility. He needs taking down a peg or two.*

She diligently kept up with his straight-to-the-point flow of words, her pen racing across the paper. She had to admire his efficiency; this office was running at peak performance. He expected the best. But it would help if his mood improved.

As she read back the last letter to his satisfaction, Mrs. Wyatt wondered if having the best of everything was her boss' problem. She was certain a woman was at the bottom of all this—*probably said no to Andrew Tracklin. It must have happened that night at the symphony, he's been acting strangely since.*

Sitting at her computer, typing up the morning's letters, she grinned. *She must be one strong woman to resist Andrew Tracklin.* Why, if she were thirty years younger he'd only have to twinkle those baby blue eyes at her and she'd swoon at his feet.

She tried to picture the woman capable of resisting her employer's charms—have to be confident, liberated, drop-dead gorgeous . . . or maybe not. Perhaps she was shy, timid, overwhelmed by his slick charm.

As she printed the final copies and checked them for accuracy, she thought how things had changed since she was young. *A modern woman . . . a match for Andrew Tracklin . . . she's turned the tables on him. I wonder if she sent him flowers and an expensive piece of jewelry.* She chuckled to herself. *Serves him right.*

She'd placed orders at florists and jewelers on his behalf, recognizing the signs of an ended affair. It was so easy for men.

The serene face his secretary presented as she handed him the letters for signing puzzled Andrew Tracklin. She wasn't lecturing him. She looked downright smug.

"Any calls, Mrs. Wyatt?"

She handed him the list of morning callers. "You told me not to put anyone through unless it was urgent."

"So I did."

"Is there some important call I should be on alert for?"

He rested his chin on his palm and stared at his secretary with unseeing eyes, far away in distant thoughts.

She cleared her throat, impatient to return to her desk.

He blinked, his head jerked up.

"No, Mrs. Wyatt."

Mrs. Wyatt softly closed the office door behind her. *It's a woman, all right!*

* * *

"Julie, you sound strange. Is something wrong?"

"No, Anna. I'm packing for a trip to Philadelphia, a little muddled is all. It's wonderful to hear your voice, I've missed you."

"There's an empty chair at our table, not a day goes by that each one of us doesn't mention your name. We miss you so much."

Julie sniffled, glad Anna couldn't see the tears streaming down her cheeks. It was supposed to get easier with time, but here she was blubbering at the first mention of Desolation Sound.

"Julie, are you still there? Our connection must be faulty, I can't hear you."

"I'm here, Anna. Where are you calling from?"

"We're in Powell River. I've had my final x-rays and the results are good, the bones have healed, circulation is strong, and all that's left is a little stiffness when I overdo things."

"Wonderful news!"

"Has Andrew Tracklin been to see you?"

"No. I made a presentation to the Tracklin's board of directors and convinced them to cancel spraying for all time. But there was no sign of Andrew. Why do you ask?"

"Julie, that's wonderful about the spraying being canceled. Andrew came looking for you the day you left, furious you weren't here. He asked me over and over if you'd left a message for him. He was leaving on business for Japan and demanded your address. He was going to see you before he left."

"Well, he didn't. I guess he changed his mind."

"Julie, you should've seen him. He would find you; I had no doubt. He swore it often enough."

"I haven't heard from him, Anna."

"That's strange, Julie. He flew out of here like a man possessed, muttering about unfinished business and setting you straight."

"I haven't seen him, Anna, no visits, no phone calls, not even a postcard."

"Odd . . . I was so sure."

"Give it up, Anna. The clock has struck midnight for that nymph from the backwoods, and her pumpkin turned into a sports car."

"Don't talk like that. You're the same sweet, caring sister you've always been, city or country, career or not. The man's not stupid."

Julie smiled. Her mild-mannered sister was fierce when defending her family.

"Thanks, Anna. I appreciate your confidence. But this time it won't help. The man may not be stupid but he only saw me in unusual circumstances. Now his dream has vanished."

Anna grimaced, grinding her teeth. Her little sister could be so stubborn, and so blind. The man was desperate to see her. Something must have gone wrong. Perhaps he's in hospital, maybe a plane crash; something kept him from getting to Julie.

"Have you thought of contacting him?"

"You mean me . . . phone Andrew Tracklin?"

"Why not?"

She couldn't come up with a good answer. It hadn't occurred to her to make the first move.

"Think about it, Julie. Trust me on this. Find his number in the phone book and give him a call. I can't imagine why he hasn't contacted you. Maybe he's deathly ill or had a serious accident."

The subject of Andrew Tracklin was dropped as the two sisters exchanged the past month's news. It was only as Anna hung up the telephone that the thought crossed her mind. *I wonder if I copied the address wrong?*

Julie packed her most somber business suit for the conference in Philadelphia. She was representing Northern

Chemicals and would be addressing a gathering of chemists and engineers to describe her company's successful venture and future prospects. She'd been so apathetic about her work lately, maybe spending time with fellow chemists who understood what she was talking about would restore the spark.

She folded her gray skirt and matching jacket into her suitcase. Even with her education and work experience, it was hard to be seen as a serious scientist. Looking feminine and attractive equated with being dimwitted and unqualified. Appearances could be so deceiving.

She went to bed with that thought in her mind. Her appearance at Desolation Sound had deceived a dashing pilot with eyes the color of sun-dappled sky. She was paying for that deception.

She punched her pillows, tossed about trying to get comfortable. She needed her sleep, she had five days of meetings to attend.

But sleep was elusive, the deception weighed heavy on her conscience.

The sleek black Jaguar sped along Vancouver's streets, suddenly screeched to a skidding halt, made a hasty right turn on the red light, circled the block of trendy shops, restaurants and galleries, then reappeared at the far end of the street, moving slowly, searching for a parking spot.

"That picture in the window . . . where did you get it?"

The dapper gallery owner wasn't accustomed to huge men built like bodybuilders crashing their way into his art gallery and shouting at him. Galleries were for quiet appreciation, not noisy demands.

"I'm a sales agent for the painter."

"Where did you get it?" The voice was insistent and loud and the man glared at him as if he'd committed a crime. The poor man stared, confused and bewildered, not knowing how to answer this madman.

"How did it get here? Answer me, damn you!"

"It was delivered."

"By whom? Cough it out man! Who delivered it?"

"A young woman . . . my contact with the painters."

"How do you get in touch with her?"

"I don't."

"Give me her address."

"I don't have it, sir."

"How the hell do you deal with a contact if you can't contact her?"

The gallery owner sniffed his displeasure, adjusted the gold cuff link on his fine silk shirt, and gave a quelling look to the irate customer in his shop.

"I send all correspondence to a post office box in Powell River. The painter lives in a remote area along the coast."

"I know where she lives. Are you deaf, man? Where's the woman who delivered the painting?"

"If you'll calm yourself, sir, I'll repeat what I've already told you. I don't know. I have no dealings with her except when she brings in paintings on behalf of the artists."

"Wrap it up."

"Wrap what, sir?"

"The painting. I'm taking it with me. Now!"

"I'm afraid not, sir. This is a place of business. I don't release works of art to anyone but the owner."

"It's sold?"

"No, sir. But it is for sale."

"It's sold! No one is having a picture of my Julie—no one but me. Do you hear?"

"It would be hard not to, sir, you're bellowing loud enough to be heard down the block."

"Get it out of the window."

"Will that be cash or charge, sir?"

"Get it, I say."

"Until it's paid for, sir, it stays where it is."

Angered, the deranged customer growled at the pompous

little man, pulled out his credit card and slammed it down beside the vase of autumn chrysanthemums, almost toppling them.

"Do you wish to know the price?"

"I don't give a damn about the price! I want that painting. It's mine."

The gallery owner raised dark eyebrows, scrutinizing this unlikely art lover. "Perhaps you'd like to know more about the artist, the location."

"Damn it, man! Double your asking price. Just sell me that painting and hand it over."

The startled man quickly processed the sale and unlocked the display cabinet, handing over the melancholy portrait.

An amazing transformation overcame the nasty customer as he held the painting at arm's length and smiled. His rigid stance relaxed, the creased brow eased, his clenched fists turned into gentle hands holding the frame reverently, gazing at the portrait with soulful eyes that only a moment ago were shooting daggers. "My Julie," he sighed. His yearning expression matched the longing sadness of the woman's face in the painting.

The gallery owner handed back the credit card that had accepted the exorbitant sales price. "Your card, sir."

Jostled out of his trance, the customer pocketed the card, but refused to release his grasp on the painting as the man reached out to wrap it.

"Forget the packaging. I'll take it like this."

Having noted his name from his credit card, the gallery owner bowed from his waist. "Very good, Mr. Tracklin. We represent many B.C. artists, perhaps you'd like to see the rest of our exhibit."

He was left talking to empty space as the tall man in the business suit folded himself into a pricey sports car parked at the curb, his newly purchased work of art placed lovingly on the passenger seat beside him.

He shook his head and adjusted the chrysanthemums in the vase.

"Strangest sale I ever made."

Julie had plenty of time to mull Anna's phone call on the plane flight. Andrew came after her.

What harm would calling him do?

What could she lose?

My pride. That was long gone. She didn't feel very proud about holding back the whole truth about herself. She wouldn't blame him for being angry and refusing to speak to her.

She settled the argument with herself by the time the plane landed. She'd pick up the telephone and call him. What was the worst that could happen?

He'd refuse her call.

It was worth a try.

It wasn't until the second day of the conference that Julie worked up enough nerve to punch in the long distance number for Tracklin's head office that directory assistance had given her the day she arrived.

"Tracklin's. May I help you?"

"I'd like to speak to Mr. Tracklin."

"Which Mr. Tracklin would that be, ma'am?"

"Andrew Tracklin."

"I'll put you through to his secretary."

Julie exhaled a long breath. Now was not the time to lose her courage. She could feel her heart pounding and the rehearsed speech evaporating from her mind.

"Mr. Tracklin's office. Mrs. Wyatt speaking. May I help you?"

"May I speak with Mr. Tracklin, please?"

"I'm sorry, Miss. He isn't in his office. Would you like to leave a number and he can return your call?"

"No . . . no . . . I . . ."

"Would you like to leave a message?"

"No . . . mm . . . just tell him Julie called."

The connection was severed before Mrs. Wyatt could get any more information. By the delicate, uncertain sound of the woman's voice, she guessed this was the woman her boss was working himself into a state over.

She noted the time of the call and placed the message on his desk.

Fireworks were about to erupt, but she was nonchalantly typing when her boss returned to the office, barely looking up to nod as he strode through to his desk.

She began counting to ten and waited.

At five, he stormed up to her desk, slapped the message in front of her and roared, "That's all! Haven't you learned to take proper messages in all these years? What else did she say?"

"Not a thing, sir."

"Did you get her phone number?"

"No sir."

"Why the hell not?"

"I asked, but she didn't wish to leave a number. There's no need to shout at me."

"I'll shout if I want!"

"Fine. But it won't help find her." Looking up at her enraged employer, Mrs. Wyatt tempted fated by adding, "She had a pleasant voice."

That brought him back to his senses. Very quietly, he muttered, "She has a beautiful voice."

But the raving boss was instantly back. "Get the telephone company, have the call traced. Immediately, Mrs. Wyatt. I'll be in my office. Find out where she was phoning from."

He stormed out, the windows rattling from the force of the door crashing behind him.

* * *

"Philadelphia? What do you mean, Philadelphia? What's she doing in Philadelphia?"

Mrs. Wyatt shrugged. "That's where the call was traced to. I dialed the number, it's a hotel." She placed the information on his desk. "I didn't know who to ask for. Perhaps you'd like to make the call yourself."

She had no idea that he didn't know the woman's full name. No hotel would put through a call for Julie when the caller only knew her first name.

She was stunned by the misery on the face that stared back at her. She waited, expected further instructions, an explanation, a howl of anguish. He looked more than a man scorned; he looked like a warrior vanquished.

"Maybe she'll call back."

His head slumped onto his hands. "I hope so, Mrs. Wyatt. I hope so. If you hear her voice, keep her on the line. I don't care what excuse you have to use. I'll keep this cell phone with me at all times." He scribbled the number for his secretary. "Put her call through immediately."

She opened her mouth to speak.

"Immediately, Mrs. Wyatt. Disrupt any meeting, wherever I am, whatever I'm doing, put her call through. Got that?"

Mrs. Wyatt saluted. "Got that."

He grinned at his secretary. "Next time I should try sending flowers."

She smiled. She knew all along it was a woman.

On his way home to his False Creek townhouse, his cell phone secure in his inside jacket pocket, Andrew fished out the address Anna had given him so many weeks before.

It was worth another try.

Julie was in Vancouver to deliver those paintings to the gallery. This Beach Road address might offer some clue.

For the second time, that polished black car pulled up before the prestigious apartment building.

"Good afternoon, sir."

"May I see the young lady in 912?"

"I'm afraid not, sir."

"Is waiting until she gets home an option?"

"No sir."

This time he removed his business card and wrote on the back: *Julie, I must see you. Andrew.*

He stared at the doorman through narrowed eyes, handing him the card. "Inform her Andrew Tracklin called."

"Very good, sir."

The inscrutable doorman revealed not a glimmer of emotion.

It wasn't until the sleek car pulled back into the west end traffic, that he smiled. *Persistent. Good quality. Miss Marantse deserves the best.*

After a successful trip, Julie unpacked her suitcase and checked the messages on her answering machine.

"Hi Julie. It's Jason. Head office was impressed by your presentation in Philadelphia. Thought you'd like to know. Looks like promotion time for you."

Julie pressed the play button and listened to the rest of her messages. Her photos were in. The bank wanted to discuss term deposits with her. Would she donate money to the wilderness committee?

She rewound the tape, had a quick shower, then put on her jogging pants and an old sweatshirt. The day was cool but she needed fresh air and exercise. A week in an air-conditioned convention center followed by a stuffy plane flight, left her longing for the feel of sea breeze and a chance to stretch her legs.

She slipped out the main entrance without checking her mailbox. Julie waved to Larkin. He was giving parking directions to some visitors to the building. She set a steady, rhythmic pace, jogging along the beach path, inhaling the salty tang of ocean air. Fallen leaves crunched underfoot and her exhaled breath left steamy clouds in the frosty autumn air.

Chapter Ten

Next day, the Jaguar pulled up before the doorman once again.

"Good afternoon, sir."

"May I see the young lady in 912?"

"I'll announce you, sir." He took a cell phone from his pocket and punched in a series of numbers.

"Yes?"

"A gentleman is here, Miss. A Mr. Tracklin."

After a long pause, "Send him up, Larkin."

The doorman extended his hand. "If you'll give me your keys, sir, I'll park your car in the underground lot."

The surprised driver surrendered his keys, stepped out of his car, and walked through the glass door held open for him. He had waited a full week for this to happen, and now he was astounded and unprepared.

"The elevator is straight ahead, sir. The apartment you want is on the ninth floor, facing the sea."

Silently, the elevator shot him up nine stories before he had time to register the deep pile of the carpet or the tasteful surroundings, or question Julie living in such style.

A brass knocker graced the solid door marked 912, a brass plate engraved J. MARANTSE, beneath the knocker.

Andrew stiffened, steely-blue eyes glaring at the name plate. His hand clenched into a fist, tightened, then released. Now here, he feared what he'd find on the other side of the door.

Marantse was the connection; she works for him. That explains his information about Desolation Sound. What was she to Marantse—secretary, housekeeper, mistress? Secretaries and housekeepers don't live in. His frown deepened into a scowl, his fist again tightened and released.

He squared his shoulders, raised his chin, and reached tentative fingers to lift the brass knocker, then let it fall with a thump.

Approaching steps, then the door opened.

He froze, speechless, staring, his face a mask of cool composure but his heart beating frantically. He wasn't ready for this. It was Julie—but not as he'd seen her, or remembered her. Her soft green dress fell in gentle folds, nipped in at her narrow waist, caressed curving hips, and stopped at her knees, revealing shapely stockinged legs and delicate ankles. Those he recognized. The rest was a Julie he never imagined—elegant, refined, a sophisticated woman wearing designer clothes as though she'd never worn anything else.

Her dark eyes looked startled under those long lashes. Her hair, no longer wildly curly, framed her flawless face, short and tamed, with only a hint of curl across her forehead. His gaze settled on her lips, moist and pink with lipstick.

Lost for words, questions racing through his mind, he hated the thought she lived with Marantse. This wasn't the way a housekeeper dressed. No wonder she was secretive about her work.

"You live here?"

"Yes. Would you like to come in?"

He hid his chaotic thoughts well and appeared the competent man, fully in control.

She led him into a bright living room, colorful and inviting, with the kind of comfortable furniture that welcomed you to sink into its soft cushions. A huge window overlooking the sea filled the room with light reflected by the expanse of ocean stretching out across the bay. Julie motioned him to sit in a large armchair near the window.

He looked as she remembered him—dashingly handsome, tall and slender, his soft gray suit molded to his muscular frame. Only his blue eyes looked haunted, and there was a lean, gaunt tension about his face. No laughing sparkle or teasing grin lightened the glare taking in her every breath.

She didn't know where to begin. The tense silence between them finally forced her to speak.

"How did you find me?"

"Anna gave me your address."

"Did she tell you anything about me?"

"Only your address."

Julie lowered her eyes, not knowing what to say, heart racing at the sight of him, afraid he was looking for a woman he only imagined.

Wriggling in her chair, fidgeting with her hands clasped in her lap, courage woefully absent she avoided his eyes, not saying any of the things she wanted to say. He looked furious.

He noted her nervous movements, her downcast head. She was ill at ease and he wondered why. What was so shameful she had to keep it secret? He waited for her to lift her eyes to meet his. But she didn't.

When he finally spoke, it jolted through her, that deep penetrating voice quivered from her ears to her toes.

"What's your relationship with Marantse?"

Her head jerked up and her wide brown eyes made contact with the accusing face that studied her so solemnly.

"What . . . ?" That was not a question she had expected to hear.

"Are you his mistress?" His voice was louder, trembling with anger or some other emotion.

Like sunshine breaking through clouds, Julie smiled. Was that all he wanted to know? Her furrowed brow smoothed, her mouth turned up at the corners, her face lit with a secret knowledge. That question was the easiest to answer. She got up from her chair, crossed the carpet softly to stand beside his armchair, and bent down to whisper quietly into his ear, "We're inseparable, Marantse and I."

His fingers dug into the arms of the upholstered chair. His stricken look made her take pity on him and hasten to explain.

"The J on the nameplate stands for Julie. My name is Julie Marantse."

For a moment he didn't move, the lines across his forehead softened, his fingers ceased biting into the armchair, he turned his head and stared into her face. She smelled heavenly, like spring flowers on an ocean breeze.

Sunshine broke through the clouds. The smile spread gradually, glinting from his eyes, radiating from his mouth, and warming the room like dawn after a long dark night. He couldn't stop himself. He leaned forward and kissed her lips.

Soft pink traces of lipstick outlined the masculine lips that sighed with relief and smiled at her possessively.

Julie knew an accounting had to be made, explanations given, but for now it was enough to be here with Andrew. He swallowed and caught his breath. He had never been so glad to hear someone's full name.

"You wrote that report? You're a chemical engineer?"

"Yes." Her voice was barely a whisper. He stared at her so intensely, she feared her breathing would stop and she'd faint dead away. Her troubled eyes seemed to fill her whole face.

Her nervousness burbled out in a tumble of words. "It

got out of hand . . . I meant to tell you . . . it was so important not to let spraying ruin Anna's life."

He stroked her cheek with the back of his hand.

"All this is yours?"

She stared up into his compelling blue eyes. She nodded. Was this when he exploded in anger?

A full smile spread across his face, crinkling the corners of his eyes. He really was devastating when he smiled.

"You're at home here . . . in the city?"

She nodded again. She held her breath, waiting.

The aggravating man didn't say another word. He left her stranded like a man overboard without a lifeline. Were her dreams false hopes?

Why was he looking so satisfied, as though he'd solved the mystery of the universe? What was he plotting?

He fixed her with those impenetrable blue eyes. His voice was that of a schoolteacher catching a student getting into mischief. "Would you care to explain?"

"Explain?"

"Yes. I think you have a lot of explaining to do. How is it the nature-loving, rustic woman lives in an elegant apartment, writes scientific reports like a pro, and never made the merest mention that she had a city life?"

"Well, I do love nature . . . simple life . . . sailing . . . that part wasn't a lie."

"I'm aware of that. You can't fake a love for sailing."

"I wasn't faking."

"No. But you concealed a great deal about yourself. You weren't exactly telling the truth."

Crimson flushed her cheeks. He was right. How could she explain not telling him about herself, letting him believe only what he saw? She couldn't explain it to herself.

"I got carried away pretending . . . then one thing led to another . . . and . . ."

"And?"

"I didn't want to let you down . . . not be the woman you wanted me to be."

"Oh, Julie. If only you'd spoken up. I saw you loved your sister's family . . . and the lifestyle. I suspected there was more to you than the eye could see."

Anna had warned her; she'd have to pay for her deception. She peered up expecting a stern lecture on honesty, and then a final exit. He held her gaze with the same inquisitive look he'd had the first time she saw him in the patch of brambles. He was waiting for an answer.

"I wasn't telling an untruth . . . I just left out a few things."

His laughter was unsettling. She squirmed and turned her head to look out across the water of English Bay.

"Well, my love, now I'd like you to fill in 'the few things' you left out."

His voice was reasonable not critical. That made it harder. Anger was easier to deal with. It was impossible to lose your temper and shout back at someone who was being so kind, and called you 'my love.'

He deserved an explanation.

"I told you I work . . . I'm a chemical engineer." Once started, the words came out in a rush. "I didn't mean to mislead you . . . you wanted me to be the unrestrained spirit . . . an unspoiled illusion . . . I didn't want to disappoint you."

A long sigh punctuated her words. "And it was only for a few months. Once I left Desolation Sound, I was sure we'd never meet again."

He took both her hands in his and looked down at her bowed head.

"Look at me, Julie." She cautiously raised her chin, expecting the worst. "When I returned and you were gone, I was livid. I knew you were more than the unpolished waif, working her fingers to the bone, remote and isolated."

He stroked her soft, manicured fingers with slow deliberation.

"You didn't trust me enough to tell the truth."

Her mouth opened, ready to speak, but he shushed her lips with a gentle finger.

"I thought we lived very different lives—yours, on a windswept shore and mine, in an air-conditioned office. But I wanted to introduce you to my family, to my life here in Vancouver. I hoped we had enough in common to overcome the differences. But you vanished."

A hush settled over the room. She hadn't known. She wished she could begin again, those months out of time, the misunderstandings. What a fool she'd been.

Her woebegone face mirrored her feelings; tears shimmered in her velvet brown eyes, blurring her vision.

"I suspected a secret. The wild woman in tattered shorts captivated me."

He warmed her through with a devastating smile. "I'm also captivated by the poised woman in this high-rise."

"You are?'

He leaned forward and stilled her parted lips with his own.

"I am."

A lock of sun-streaked hair slipped forward, and as he lifted his hand to brush it off his forehead, Julie's hand brushed his as she reached out to do the same thing. Their fingers touched and neither pulled away. He lifted her hand to his lips and gently kissed it.

Julie's heart raced at his touch and the warmth in his eyes. She felt light enough to float.

His gorgeous smile didn't help her fluttering pulse. He was taking in the sight and feel of her; he couldn't get enough. She hadn't vanished, never wanting to set eyes on him again. Seeing her once more was better than he'd hoped. He wasn't going to let her disappear this time.

"Join me for dinner tonight?"

Oh how she wanted to accept that invitation. But she couldn't.

"I have to work—four o'clock to midnight."

"You work nights?"

"A chemical plant operates twenty-four hours a day; sometimes it's my turn on evening shift."

He looked terribly disappointed, unwilling to let her vanish so soon after finding her. His voice was quiet, but his eyes held hers so possessively, she wondered if he was going to command her to quit her job. He didn't.

"I put off searching you out for so long . . . so many wasted days and weeks . . . so much loneliness and despair. Now I want you to myself, no distractions, no interruptions, no vanishing acts."

She heard the edge of steel in his voice. The powerful Mr. Tracklin was back. But he smiled at her with such tenderness, she smiled back, digesting his words.

"May I drive you to work?"

"I'd be stranded beside the river, in the dark of night, no bus, no way home."

"I'll be there to bring you home."

She gave him a sensible look. "I'm poor company at midnight."

"I'll risk it."

She relaxed then, and smiled at his eagerness, touched by his determination. She couldn't think of anything more wonderful than having Andrew waiting for her at midnight.

"Thank you . . . but don't say I didn't warn you."

Pleased to at last have Julie beside him, Andrew drove slowly through the city streets, chiding himself for having believed a wild flower couldn't flourish in the city. Here she was, as enchanting as ever, at ease in this rush-hour traffic. It took willpower to concentrate on his driving and keep his eyes on the road; they kept straying to the woman in the passenger seat. She was heavenly . . . and real, no figment of his imagination.

Not needing to conceal her real self, Julie shared opinions on restaurants, movies, and music. They agreed on many things, the conversation smooth and rapid, never ceasing as they crossed the Oak Street Bridge over one arm of the Fraser River and continued south through the brightly lit concrete tunnel under a second arm of the river. With so much lost time to catch up, Andrew wasn't in a hurry to have this journey end and be forced to leave her.

He couldn't prevent the inevitable, no matter how slowly he drove. The road followed the riverbank and reached the locked gates of the chemical plant.

Being watched warily by the security guard, Andrew opened the car door for Julie. She looked up into a puzzling expression, not that of the confident helicopter pilot but more the tearful look of Simon when she was leaving.

"This is where we say good-bye." She motioned to the chain-link fence. "It's as far as you can come."

Light was fading, as Andrew looked along the road to the chemical plant, looming up like a brightly painted, many-legged creature in the cleared acreage.

"How do you get the rest of the way?"

"There's a bicycle."

Good-bye was not what he wanted to say, not now, not ever. One hand circled her small waist and drew her toward him, the other tilted her head back. He placed a kiss on her lips . . . long and sweet.

He saw the security guard closely watching from the corner of his eye. Reluctantly he loosened his hold.

"Are there men guarding you everywhere? First Simon, then your doorman, and now this guard. Will I ever be alone with you?"

Julie heard the impatience in his voice and felt the pain of having to leave him standing here. She must part quickly or she'd never be able to pull herself away.

Julie stood on tiptoe, wrapped her arms around his neck and kissed him, letting there be no doubt she, too, wanted to stay.

"See you at midnight," she whispered, then slipped through the gates, greeted the guard, put on her hard hat, and pedaled off down the road, before she had a chance to think or look back.

Delighted by that parting kiss, Andrew watched from behind locked gates until she was out of sight.

He loved her.

Retracing his route to Vancouver, no one saw the blissful expression on Andrew's face or was party to the plans forming in his mind.

Julie had cut a swath through his life, like the trail behind a tornado. He could never go back to his pilot's life of carefree indulgence. The gentle woman who hid her soft brown eyes against his shoulder in a tiny movie theater was an engineer in the city. The lively spirit at home in the serenity of the rugged British Columbia wilderness was equally at home in the glass and concrete jungle of high-rises. Was it so surprising? She was poised and comfortable aboard his sailboat; but then, she was poised and comfortable at The Empress Hotel. He should have guessed. But he never dared hope.

He'd wanted it to be true; he'd been afraid to hope. Sharing her love of the outdoors, he could now share his enjoyment of the city, as well.

He laughed aloud, aiming his car toward the exclusive Oakridge shops. *Look at me now. My old flight crew wouldn't recognize me; the pilot who avoided commitment was willing to give up his freedom and step into the family business, and with eyes and heart for only one woman.* He grinned at the irony.

Those things once so important didn't matter when he thought of Julie. City or country, career or dependence, wealth or poverty—all those sensible considerations were wiped out at the mere sight of her. He'd fallen for a bewitching breath of fresh air. It felt wonderful.

Heads turned as he walked into the expensive shopping mall, an eye-catching man with a sense of purpose, vibrantly alive and his face wreathed with the joy of it.

His purchase made, he sped out of the Oakridge parking lot headed for his parents' home. He hadn't seen them since returning from Japan; his father was awaiting news of the lumber negotiations. He had other news for them too.

Mrs. Wilson opened the door. "Your parents are expecting you, in the den."

She didn't bustle straight back to the kitchen, but paused, curious about his starry-eyed look.

"Is something wrong?"

"No, Mrs. Wilson. Something is very right."

That was all she could get out of him. She shook her head, adjusted her apron, and turned back to the kitchen. "Something's afoot, mark my words." She'd seldom seen Andrew looking dreamy. It could only be one of two things—either he'd been hit on the head, or he was in love.

She rolled out the piecrust with firm strokes. "Well, it's about time."

The strange sparkle in their son's eyes and the radiant smile on his face didn't go unnoticed by his parents, either. It was unlike him to have been drinking so early in the day.

"Successful trip?"

"Everything you hoped for."

He answered his father's questions, but Rebecca Tracklin suspected more than business was on her son's mind. He hadn't sat down, but instead he paced back and forth in front of the fireplace, stroking his chin and staring vacantly into the room without seeing either of his parents.

"Was there something else you wanted to tell us?"

Andrew stopped and sat down suddenly on the sofa beside his mother. "I've met the most wonderful woman."

Robert Tracklin roared, "Heaven help us! Not another nightclub singer?"

Andrew's smile made his father fear he'd lost his senses. He sat bolt upright in his armchair, his face pinched in worry. "This family doesn't need another brazen hussy!"

Mrs. Tracklin took a much calmer approach. "Tell us about her, dear. Did you meet in Japan?"

"A geisha!" her husband muttered, wringing his hands.

"We met on Desolation Sound."

He paused, not aware of his father having fits across the room.

"A fishwife!"

His mother prompted him back to the subject. "What is she like?"

"She's incredible."

Realizing this conversation was revealing nothing, except Andrew was smitten, Mrs. Tracklin suggested they move to the dining room.

Andrew babbled through dinner about Julie. It seemed logical to him; he'd thought of nothing else for weeks.

His father was still imagining the worst possible daughter-in-law. "A dance hall girl! That's all we need!"

"Robert, for heavens sake, stop interrupting. Andrew wants to tell us about Julie."

As Mrs. Wilson served each course, she left shaking her head. The Tracklin men were both dithering off on topics of their own, and poor Mrs. Tracklin was trying to make sense of it. It was the most muddled dinner conversation she'd ever heard.

Robert Tracklin stopped listing his worst nightmares, his head jerked upward and he stared at his son. "Repeat that!" he bellowed.

"I'm going to marry her."

Silence descended, as if all the air was sucked out of the room. Mr. and Mrs. Tracklin stared at their son, speechless.

He was delirious and they were skeptical, especially after David's choice of wife.

No congratulations were offered. None seemed appropriate. Andrew smiled into space with the glazed eyes of a lunatic.

The distant ticking of a clock and the breathing of the three people at the table were the only sounds.

That is, until Robert Tracklin pushed back his chair and wandered to the drinks cabinet to pour himself a stiff brandy.

He was back to mumbling. Rebecca Tracklin rose from the table and caught her husband's parting grumble.

"Gold digger," was the last word she heard before she fainted.

Like a sleepwalker, Julie worked the late shift, her thoughts on a pair of lovely blue eyes and a man who sent shivers through her at the memory. Luckily no technical difficulties required her attention.

The story hadn't ended when she left Desolation Sound. Andrew hadn't forgotten her. He'd cared enough to search her out even when he thought she was a housekeeper, or worse, for someone else.

She dared not hope. But he had come.

Julie counted the seconds until midnight. No man had set her heart fluttering and her head swimming by smiling at her. Andrew Tracklin did.

Nothing short of a major explosion in the chemical plant could draw her wandering thoughts away from him.

Finally, the hands of the clock crept closer to midnight. Julie greeted her night shift replacement with unusual enthusiasm, jumped onto a bicycle, and raced to the gates.

He was there.

Her heart skipped a beat as she saw the black car waiting with a familiar tall gentleman, resplendent in black tie and evening clothes, leaning against the hood.

When she pedaled out of the darkness into the pool of light cast by the security guard's hut, Andrew flashed that dazzling smile and extended his arms toward her.

Julie skittered through the gate and melted into those outstretched arms. Oblivious to the security guard, the late night hour, and the cold chill in the air, their lips met.

The uniformed guard cleared his throat loudly without being heard. It wasn't until Andrew felt Julie shiver that he lifted his head.

"You're cold." He opened the car door. "Get in, the heater's on. We have an appointment to keep."

"Appointment? At this time of night?"

Andrew had slipped off his jacket and was tucking it around her shoulders. He couldn't resist kissing the side of her neck.

"Yes . . . too important to wait."

Julie snuggled into the warmth of his jacket, the scent of his cologne teasing her nostrils. He wouldn't tell her anything more. She was happy just to be with him.

She snoozed as he drove quickly through nearly empty streets into town, past her apartment building, and along the shore of English Bay. In the dead of night, the beach was deserted, but he saw what he was looking for, pulled to the curb and parked.

He leaned over and placed a gentle kiss on Julie's closed eyelids. "We're here."

She opened sleepy eyes, expecting to be in front of her apartment building. But his car was parked beside the beach.

All was still, deserted, no wind, no sound of traffic. The half moon cast a silver path across the undisturbed water of the bay. The moonlight reflected in Andrew's eyes, and bathed the polished black car in a shimmering light.

The broad expanse of sand stretched to the sea, broken only by logs washed up in storms and left at the high water mark for sunbathers to sit on and stretch out against.

Julie's eyes were adjusting to the dim light and she thought she saw a shadowy movement near the water, and some abandoned beach chairs, long forgotten.

Andrew took her hand and urged her out of the car, across the grass, and onto the beach, toward the moving shadow. Their feet sank into the soft sand, making their movements slow as they stepped around logs, their shoes filling with sand. The salt tang of sea air washed over them. Julie hadn't been to the water's edge in the dark of night. It was an eerie, magical place, quiet without crowds of people. Surely he didn't plan on swimming—the air was cold, and the water freezing.

His warm hand kept tight hold of hers as they neared the ocean. Those forgotten beach chairs weren't forgotten at all; they were carefully placed, either side of a table draped in white linen, at the water's edge.

An impeccably dressed waiter bent over at the waist and lit two candles whose flickering light illuminated a bowl of red roses. The waiter maintained his dignified air, even though his shoes were filling with gritty sand and the damp sea air was making his crisp linen cloth limp with moisture.

With his arm at her back, Andrew seated Julie in one of the chairs, then sat in the chair opposite her.

Speechless, Julie stared—moonlight, candles, roses—at a bottle of champagne cooling on ice. Andrew was in elegant evening clothes and she was in grubby work clothes, but it didn't seem to matter. It had an unreal quality, like a dream, but the smell of sand and sea, and the cold dampness turning her fingers blue and making her lips chatter, assured her it was real.

"Andrew, you're insane."

"No, my precious, not insane . . . in love."

He took her hand and gazed at her with such devotion, she forgot they were only blocks from the bustling city center, and she was cold and tired. She saw only the moonlight on his handsome face, felt his hand warm on hers and smelled the sweet fragrance of roses. It was better than a dream.

"We met by the sea." He dropped to one knee on the sand beside Julie, holding her hand, warming it in his, and searching her eyes. His voice thick with emotion, he continued, "and it is here by the sea I'm asking you to be my wife."

For someone never at a loss for words, Julie was suddenly stricken dumb. She must be asleep. This sort of thing only happened in dreams. Her look of disbelief, in the light of the flickering candles, would have discouraged a lesser man. But Andrew smiled, stroking her hands to warm them, and loving this gentle woman all the more. She hadn't manipulated him into this position; he was on his knees before her because he wanted to be here.

"I love you, Julie. I want you in my life, every second of every day." In spite of the deserted beach and the cold night air, she was warmed through by the gentle plea in his voice and the passion in his eyes. "Will you marry me?"

Overcome, her mind finally grasping the wondrous reality of it all, Julie slipped from her chair, threw her arms around his neck, and toppled them both into the cold sand. Before their lips met, she managed to say, "Yes, yes, yes."

The distinguished waiter, unperturbed by the couple covered in grainy bits of sand, kissing on a lonely stretch of beach in the early hours before dawn, uncorked the champagne and filled two crystal glasses. He stood silently beside the table, never raising an eyebrow or allowing any sign of emotion to cross his face.

After long moments, Andrew lifted Julie to her feet, gently brushed sand from her clothing, and handed her a glass of champagne. He lifted his glass in a toast.

"To the woman I love. May I make her as happy as she's made me."

They sipped in silence, staring out to sea, the gentle wash of waves against the shore the only sound, Andrew's arm protectively around Julie. She cuddled against him, very much in love with this man who'd brought her to a deserted beach in the middle of the night and asked her to be his wife.

Andrew turned, as if seeing the waiter for the first time. "Saunders, she said yes."

"Congratulations, sir." The elderly man finally smiled at his employer. He didn't need to be told the young lady's response. She had repeated it breathlessly between kisses as the sand worked its way into their hair, down their necks and into their clothes. It must be love. Nothing else would have his employer rolling about in cold, wet sand in his finest evening clothes in the middle of the night.

To assure himself he wasn't dreaming, Andrew kissed Julie once more, then ever so slightly moved back from her embrace and reached into his pocket. He removed a ring from its tiny black box and placed it on her finger. She stared transfixed, at the large diamond in a setting of rubies, glittering in the moonlight on her sandy finger.

Unable to speak, she lifted adoring eyes to his. Her love was mirrored back in his look.

"The diamond reflects your beauty, fresh and sparkling like the sea." He turned her hand in his and kissed her palm.

"And the rubies reflect your other side—the flames of passion."

Ankle deep in sand, damp hair curling around his ears, but a joyous lightness in his heart, he tenderly whispered into her ear, "Darling, I love you."

Julie only had time to slip her arms around him to keep from falling back into the sand.

He thrilled to the sound of the words she sighed against his lips. "I love you, Andrew."

Those were the words he'd waited to hear.

Chapter Eleven

The small sailboat rocked gently, at anchor in the scenic cove, the breeze pinging its rigging against the aluminum mast. A waterfall splashed down over the steep, rocky cliff rising up from the sea. Early morning fog hung low over the water and clung to the treetops, shrouding the mountain peaks in a thick blanket of white cloud. The cove was silent and secluded, miles from any sign of civilization. The first shafts of sunlight cut through the morning mist and sparkled off the white-painted hull of the lone sailboat.

Inside, the small cabin was warm and dry. Julie was vaguely aware of a comforting, gentle breath against her hair. She wriggled her shoulders and felt the firmness of Andrew's chest behind her. His arm tightened and pulled her closer.

"Good morning, my love," Andrew whispered, the scratchy roughness of his night's growth of beard tickling her neck.

Julie rolled over to look into those blue eyes that still set her head swimming.

"Good morning, darling."

"We'll never make it to Desolation Sound if we stay here all day. You're shameless, Mrs. Tracklin."

Julie's response was immediate. "Shameless? You're calling me shameless? Who kissed me like a love-starved Casanova in front of his straight-laced board of directors? That's who's shameless, Andrew Tracklin!"

"I love you," he whispered. "You know, I was upset when those men at Northern Chemicals gave you expensive lingerie as a wedding gift. I wanted to be the only man to buy you lingerie." He looked at his wife possessively. "They knew exactly what suited you, even the correct size. Tell me, how did they know such details?"

Mischief twinkled in her brown eyes. "They saw me in the showers often enough."

"In the showers?"

"With my clothes on . . . we rinsed down after spills to avoid chemical burns."

"That eases my mind." Andrew snuggled closer. "I'm not upset now. I understand they loved you and gave a gift to celebrate your feminine charm. I thought it a selfish wedding gift, just for you, but I see it was for me too."

He flashed that irresistible smile that left her breathless.

The morning sun was high in the sky and the early mist had lifted before Andrew and Julie appeared on the deck of the little sailboat. Andrew pulled up the anchor as Julie unfurled the mainsail. A brisk wind gusted, and she was anxious to see the sail full, pulling the sleek hull quickly through the water.

As Julie and Andrew shared a love of sailing, there had been no hesitation about spending their honeymoon at sea on a little boat. Even Andrew's offer of the Hawaiian holiday she'd missed, didn't change her mind. Julie wanted to be alone with the man she loved. She'd have to share him with the rest of the world soon enough. For now, she was content to gaze at him, knowing she was his wife and thrilling at the very thought of it.

Andrew sat beside her in the cockpit. "You're a fine

sailor, mate." He glanced up at the tightly filled sail. "Never an hour goes by, I don't discover one more lovable thing about you."

"You're rather prejudiced, Mr. Tracklin." Julie smiled. "I only hope to make you as happy as you make me." She leaned against the strong arm about her waist. "I love you, Andrew."

"Tell me again." He studied the soft curves of his wife nestled against his arm. "I love hearing you say that."

Soft brown eyes melted under his gaze. Julie placed a moist kiss on her husband's lips. "I love you, Andrew," she repeated.

Both his arms tightened around her, knocking the tiller from her hand. The sail began to flap noisily as the untended boat veered off course, lost speed, and bobbed idly, its sail flapping uselessly as the two occupants of the cockpit ignored the unset sail and left the boat to drift.

After several long minutes, Andrew took over the tiller and set the sailboat back on course. "We'll never reach Desolation Sound at the rate we're going." His arm pulled Julie close to his side. "I keep being distracted." He grinned down at her.

"Keep your mind on the sailing, I'll go below and make lunch." She wiggled out of his hold and disappeared down the hatchway to the galley.

As they ate in the warm afternoon sun, with the fresh ocean breeze whipping through their hair, Andrew marveled at his luck in finding the woman of his dreams. She tantalized his senses, she loved the things he did, she was bright and witty, and pampered him without ever losing her fiery independence and sparkle.

"You charmed my father." Andrew smiled. "I've never seen him so happy. After Monique said she detested 'those primitive backwoods', Father was overjoyed to hear you loved forests."

"Even when I told him he'd have to change his logging practices?"

"Even then. He was most impressed when he saw you in the research lab. He tells anyone who will listen, you're the best chemist Tracklin Industries ever employed."

"He's as prejudiced as his son."

"No, love. He's right. When Northern Chemicals accepted your resignation, they lost their greatest asset."

Julie shook her head. "I enjoyed working there but the challenge was gone. I'd rather be doing research and environmental studies for you." She ran her fingers over Andrew's bare arm. "You're very nice to work for, you know."

Andrew's watchful eyes left the sail to look at his lovely wife. "Did I tell you my father believes you could take over the Tracklin Empire and run it single-handed, more successfully than either of his sons?"

Julie laughed. "You're exaggerating."

"Not me. You've also changed his mind about Tracklin women having careers."

"I thought he was just glad I'm not a nightclub singer."

Andrew chuckled. "My parents both love you, Julie."

"It was generous of them to offer us their family home. I hope they weren't offended when I said I'd rather live in your townhouse."

"They weren't offended, darling, only surprised. They love your simple honesty." He kissed the tip of her nose. "And your unquestionable good taste in marrying their youngest son."

"You conceited oaf! For that, you wash up and I'll take over the tiller."

"Aye, aye, captain." Andrew saluted crisply. He disappeared into the galley, only to pop his head through the hatch and call back, "I love you."

Julie blew him a kiss and settled back with the tiller in her hand.

Who'd have thought three months spent on Desolation Sound would have ended like this?